"Jacinta, I'v̶̶̶̶̶̶̶̶̶̶̶̶̶̶̶̶̶̶̶̶̶̶ ever since ̶̶̶̶̶̶̶ ̶̶̶̶̶ you.

Paul continued. "I couldn't sleep for wondering what your pretty mouth would feel like under mine...."

Dazzled, she sighed, and he took what he wanted, filling her with his taste—male, dark and mysterious—overwhelming her with expertise, summoning her hidden wildness in response to his passionate mastery.

When at last the kiss ended, they were both breathing erratically, and he surveyed her tender mouth with eyes that were narrowed and lit from within, purposeful and determined on conquest.

Desire clutched at her heart. In a soft, tentative voice she said his name, loving the sound of it on her lips, shaping her mouth to his liking, to her need. "Paul," she breathed....

Dear Reader,

It is the happiest of omens that the publication of my fiftieth book, **A Forbidden Desire**, should coincide with Harlequin's fiftieth anniversary. It's been a long and pleasant association, and I wish everyone at Harlequin and all our readers a very special celebration.

Because so many readers have asked over the years, "But what about Paul?" I've given this happy ending to the man who lost Aura to Flint in **Dark Fire**. Although red-headed, too, Jacinta is quite different from Paul's lost love, just as he has altered in the years since Aura married his best friend. **A Forbidden Desire** brings their stories to a conclusion, although there is always a chance that you might catch glimpses of them in future books!

Thank you all very much for your support. I hope you enjoy the books that are still on their way as much as I have enjoyed writing them for you. If you'd like to contact me, write to:

Robyn Donald
P.O. Box 18240 Glen Innes
Auckland, New Zealand

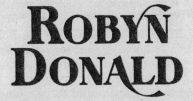

ROBYN DONALD

A Forbidden Desire

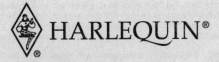

HARLEQUIN®

TORONTO • NEW YORK • LONDON
AMSTERDAM • PARIS • SYDNEY • HAMBURG
STOCKHOLM • ATHENS • TOKYO • MILAN • MADRID
PRAGUE • WARSAW • BUDAPEST • AUCKLAND

ISBN 0-373-12012-5

A FORBIDDEN DESIRE

First North American Publication 1999.

PROLOGUE

He refused to look across the crowd of people dancing beneath the intense, dark Fijian sky, but a frown half hid his hard blue eyes. He resented this awareness, this almost psychic summons, mainly because he was accustomed to thinking of himself as a restrained man, easily able to control the emotions that prowled in the cage he'd fashioned for them five years ago.

For some reason, tall, slim Jacinta Lyttelton rattled the bars of that cage. It didn't help that she was completely unaware of her power, or that he didn't know why the hell she possessed it.

Ignoring a woman who'd been trying to catch his eye for the past four days, he let his gaze roam to the pillars on the edge of the dance floor.

Heat gathered inside him. Yes, there she was, clad in one of the neat, not quite fashionable dresses she wore in the evening. She was standing alone and watching the dancers, looking interested rather than wistful.

The day before, as he'd sat talking to her mother in the shade of the leaning coconut palms, the same insistent tug at his senses had pulled his gaze away from the older woman's thin, lined face and along the hot white coral sand.

'There's Jacinta,' Mrs Lyttelton had said, smiling, her face alight with pleasure.

To his dazzled, suddenly feral eyes Jacinta had appeared as an embodiment of the fecund extravagance of the tropics, a glowing, sumptuous creature whose hair collected and intensified the sun's rays, a woman gleaming in the soft, humid air like a spirit of fire and desire.

An urgent hunger had slowed and thickened his blood. Although he'd tried to summon his usual ironic detachment to combat it, the violent physical reaction swamped both will-power and discipline.

He'd been disappointed and relieved when she got closer and the fiery goddess turned into an almost plain woman, tall, too thin, her breasts hidden by a large, faded cotton shirt, only her long, lightly tanned legs hinting at that promise of hidden passion.

Watching her now, he felt his gut clench and his body spring to painful life as he was gripped by the unmistakable burgeoning of desire. Thank God the torches that flamed around the dance floor cast enough shadows to hide his response.

The flaring light touched her pale skin with fire and licked with adoring incandescence across the aureole of her hair. The previous day she'd worn the thick, tumbling curls pulled back in a practical ponytail, but tonight she'd left it unharnessed, and the bright abundance shouted an invitation.

Dragging his eyes away, he concentrated his blue gaze on his hand on the table, saw with astonishment the rigid curl of his fingers as he fought for control. Within inches of those dark fingers flowers lay in artful, casual glory—vivid scarlet hibiscus, frilled and suggestive, and the cool, smooth stars of frangipani, their creamy restraint belied by the sweetly pervasive, erotic perfume. He wanted to crush them in his hands—he wanted to pick them up and heap them on a bed for her and take her on it for long, passionate hours until she surrendered completely and eagerly to his will.

A couple of hundred years ago he'd have believed that Jacinta Lyttelton had bewitched him. Oh, he'd always been susceptible to brilliant colouring, but the women he desired had invariably been beautiful, with a certain mysterious allure that excited the explorer in him.

Jacinta possessed neither. Skin of translucent ivory and big hazel eyes—even a soft, red, inviting mouth—were dominated by a straight, high-bridged nose and subdued by a round chin. Good legs and delicate ankles and wrists didn't compensate for the hollows at her collarbone, the angular body. Apart from that astonishing colouring, he thought, trying to be coolly dispassionate, she had no presence.

His bizarre reaction—the urge to carry her off to the nearest bedroom and stamp his imprint on her so starkly that she never looked at another man—was a sexual aberration, a primitive, freakish eccentricity caused by some delusion.

Which was just as well, because she had enough to deal with at the moment. One glance had told him that her wheelchair-bound mother was dying. He had no idea why mother and daughter had chosen to stay at this expensive resort hotel in Fiji at the hottest time of the year, but Mrs Lyttelton was enjoying it and the affection between mother and daughter was obvious.

His eyes narrowed as one of the hotel guests, a tall, brawny Australian with shoulders as wide as a barn door, approached the woman in the shadows.

A primal jealousy fogged his brain; he was on his feet and halfway across the room before he realised he'd moved. Even as he told himself that he was behaving like a fool he felt an unusual aggression tighten his muscles and fill him with unrepentant hostility.

The Australian didn't even see him; grinning, he said something that brought a smile to that soft red mouth, and turned to go out onto the beach.

Jacinta waved a hand and turned back to her survey of the dancers.

Relaxing his headlong pace, he watched the man go out into the dark night, but his skin was tight and the heavy, hungry need that prowled though him snarled softly, thwarted of legitimate prey. Noiselessly he walked up to her, some savage part of him enjoying the little jump she gave when she became conscious of his presence.

'Would you like to dance?' he asked, masking his emotions with the smile he knew was one of his greatest assets.

She looked startled, but after a moment said, 'Yes. Thank you.'

He wanted her to stumble, be heavy on her feet, not know the steps. But she was like the wind in his arms, a fragrant, spice-scented wind, swaying seductively through the languid flowers of the tropics, warm, flowing silkily against him.

Every cell in his body shouted in triumphal recognition. Anger at his helpless response cooled his voice. 'Is your mother not well enough to come tonight?'

'She's just tired.'

The faint huskiness beneath her voice smoothed across his skin like silk velvet. 'Is she enjoying the holiday?'

She looked swiftly at him, and then away again. The thick curls moved slightly as she nodded. 'She's having a wonderful time,' she said quietly. 'Everyone's been so kind.'

Because he couldn't trust himself to say anything that wouldn't increase her distress, he remained silent. Unfortunately that meant his mind could concentrate on the multitude of signals his rioting senses relayed—like the fact that her eyes were actually green, and that the hazel effect came from little gold flecks embedded in the cool depths...

Like the curve of her brows, slightly darker than her hair, and the deeper colour of her lashes as they lay on her skin, casting mysterious little shadows...

Like the tiny creases at the corners of her mouth that gave it an upward tilt...

Like the faint scent of her skin—pure essence of enchantment, he thought grimly.

Like the brush of her breasts across his chest, and the

sleek strength of her long legs as they negotiated an elderly couple enjoying themselves enormously doing what looked like a forties jitterbug.

Anger—sheer and hot and potent—only fuelled his runaway response. Of all things, he despised being at the mercy of his emotions; it had been five years since he'd felt such an elemental hunger, and even then he hadn't been tormented by this intense immediacy, this compulsion.

Thank God he was leaving tomorrow. Once back in New Zealand and deprived of nourishment, this obsession would starve and he'd be his own man again.

CHAPTER ONE

'My cousin Paul,' Gerard said in his pedantic way, 'is the only man I've ever known to decide that if he couldn't have the woman he loved he'd have no other.'

To hide her astonishment Jacinta Lyttelton gazed around Auckland's busy airport lounge. 'Really?'

Gerard sighed. 'Yes. Aura was exquisite, and utterly charming. They were the perfect match but she ran away with his best friend only days before the wedding.'

'Then they couldn't have been a perfect match,' Jacinta pointed out, smiling a little to show she was joking. During the nine months she'd known Gerard she'd learned that he needed such clues. He was a dear, kind man, but he didn't have much of a sense of humour.

'I don't know what she saw in Flint Jansen,' Gerard pursued, surprising her because he didn't normally gossip. Perhaps he thought some background information might smooth her way with his cousin. 'He was—I suppose he still is—a big, tough, dangerous man, bulldozing his way through life, hard-bitten enough to deal with anything that came his way. He was some sort of troubleshooter for one of the big corporations. Yet he was Paul's best friend right from school, and Paul is a very urbane man, worldly and cosmopolitan—a lawyer.'

Jacinta nodded politely. Perhaps Aura Whoever-she'd-been liked rough trade. 'Friendship can be just as mysterious as love. Your cousin and Flint must have had something in common for it to last so long.'

The same taste in women, to start with!

Her eyes followed a small Japanese child, fragile and solemn but clearly at home in such surroundings, her hand lost in that of her mother.

My biological clock, Jacinta thought wryly, must be ticking away. Twenty-nine wasn't over the hill, but occasionally she was oppressed by a feeling of being shunted quietly out of the mainstream, banished to float peacefully and dully in a backwater.

'I could never understand it,' Gerard said, for the fourth time turning the label on his cabin bag to check that he'd addressed it. 'She and Paul looked wonderful together and he worshipped her, whereas Flint—oh, well, it doesn't matter, but the whole sordid episode was incredibly hard on Paul.'

Being jilted would be incredibly hard on anyone. Jacinta nodded sympathetically.

Gerard frowned. 'He had to pick up the pieces of his life with everyone knowing and pitying him—and Paul is a proud man. He sold the house he and Aura were going to live in and bought Waitapu as a refuge—I suppose he thought he'd get some peace half an hour's drive north of Auckland—but then Flint and Aura settled only about twenty minutes away! In a vineyard!'

Jacinta composed her face into a sympathetic expression. Gerard's loyalty did him credit, and this wasn't the time to tell him that things had changed. Nowadays guilty couples didn't retreat to some far-flung part of the world and live in abject, if happy, retirement.

'When did this all happen?' she asked.

'Almost six years ago,' Gerard said in a mournful tone, fiddling with his boarding pass and passport.

Almost six years! Jacinta said mischievously, 'What about that exquisitely beautiful woman you pointed out to me in Ponsonby a couple of months ago? You didn't exactly say so, but you implied that she and Paul are very good friends.'

Gerard blinked and stood up. 'He's a normal man,' he

said austerely, 'but I doubt very much whether Paul intends to marry her. She's an actress.'

As well as being kind, loyal and pedantic, it appeared that Gerard was a snob.

A voice on the communications system announced that passengers for Air New Zealand's flight from Auckland to Los Angeles should make their way through the departure gate.

Gerard bent down and picked up his bag. 'So don't go falling in love with him,' he directed half seriously. 'Women do, and although he doesn't like hurting people he's broken hearts these last five years. Aura's defection killed some essential compassion in him, I think.'

'Don't worry,' Jacinta said dryly. 'I'm not planning to fall in love.'

'Not until you've finished your Masters,' he said, and to her astonishment bestowed a swift peck on her cheek. 'I'd better go.'

She hoped she'd concealed her startled response. 'Have a great trip, and I hope your research goes well.'

'It will, but thank you. Enjoy the summer,' he said, 'and work out exactly what you want to do for your thesis. Have you got the books?'

'Yes, and your list of suggestions to mull over.'

He nodded and turned away, tall, slightly stooped, his fair hair shining in the lights. Watching as he made his way through the people, Jacinta thought he always seemed out of place except when he was lecturing. Anyone looking at him would immediately pick him as an academic. If his projected book was a success he might turn out to be one of the youngest history professors in the country.

At the gate he turned and waved. Smiling, she waved back, waiting until he'd disappeared before turning to go down the escalator to the car park.

An hour and a half later she opened the car door just a hundred metres from a glorious beach, and unfurled her long, thin body and legs.

Sun-warmed, salt-tanged, the air slid into her lungs—
smooth as wine and just as heady. The big grey roof of a
house loomed above the dark barrier of a high, clipped
hedge—Cape honeysuckle, she noted, eyeing the orange
flowers—and the lazy mew of a gull smoothed across the
mellow sky.

New Zealand in summer; for the first time in years, anticipation coiled indolently through her. Not that it was
officially summer—November was the last month of
spring—but it had been a weary, wet, grinding winter and
she was eager for the sun.

A half-smile lifted the corners of her controlled mouth
as she unlatched the gate and walked up the white shell
path, amused at how pale her narrow feet looked. Ah, well,
a few walks along that sweep of sand she'd seen from the
hill would soon give them some colour. Although she
turned sallow in winter her skin loved summer, gilding
slowly under layers of sunscreen.

The house was huge, a white Victorian villa superbly
settled in a bower of lawns and flowery borders, sheltered
from the small breeze off the sea. The scents of the garden
and newly mown lawns were concentrated into an erotic,
drugging perfume.

She hoped that the man who owned all this appreciated
it.

'My cousin Paul,' Gerard had told her when he'd suggested she spend the summer at Waitapu, 'was born into
old money, and because he's both hard-headed and very
intelligent he's added considerably to the paternal legacy.'

Obviously. The house and the gardens bore the unmistakable sheen of affluence.

A bead of sweat gathered on each of Jacinta's temples.
Before leaving town she'd clipped back the hair that
reached halfway down her back, but during the drive the
curly, slippery tresses had oozed free. Tucking a bright

ginger strand behind one ear, she walked up three steps onto a wide, grey-painted wooden verandah and knocked at the door before turning to admire the gardens more closely.

She must look madly out of place here, Jacinta thought wryly, dressed in clothes without a vestige of style. And although she was tall enough to be a model she hadn't been granted a model's grace.

Her green-gold gaze roamed across the felicitous mixture of trees and shrubs, lingering on the slim grey trunks of a giant cabbage tree, each smooth branch topped by a sunburst of thin leaves. At its feet nasturtiums and Californian poppies struck sparks off each other.

The soft wind of the door opening dragged her smiling attention away from a gaudy orange and black monarch butterfly. With the smile still lingering, she turned. 'Hello, I'm Jacinta Lyttelton...'

The words dried on her tongue. She knew that handsome face—the strong jaw and arrogant cheekbones—as well as her own. The intervening months hadn't dimmed the brilliance of those eyes, a blue so intense they blazed with the colour and fire of sapphires. Yet in spite of that clarity they were oddly difficult to read.

Suddenly aware that the trousers she wore were five years old and had been cheap to start with, and that her tee-shirt had faded to a washed-out blue that did nothing for her, Jacinta realised she was standing with her jaw dangling. Clamping it shut, she swallowed, and tried to repulse a sudden, insistent warning of fate advancing inexorably, mercilessly on its way, crushing everything in its path.

'Welcome to Waitapu, Jacinta.' His deep, flexible voice wove magic, conjured darkly enchanted dreams that had dazzled her nights for months.

Fortunately her numbed brain jolted into action long enough to provide her with the location of their previous meeting.

Fiji.

The lazy, glorious week she and her mother had spent on a tiny, palm-shadowed resort island. One night he'd asked her to dance, and she'd been horrified by her fierce, runaway response to the nearness of his lean, big body. When the music had stopped he'd thanked her gravely and taken her to the room she had shared with her mother before, no doubt, rejoining the seriously glamorous woman he was on holiday with.

And for too many weeks afterwards Jacinta had let herself drift off to sleep on the memory of how it had felt to be held in those strong arms, and the faint, evocative fragrance that had owed nothing to aftershave—the essence of masculinity...

An embarrassing flash of colour stained her high cheekbones.

Damn, she thought helplessly. How unfair that this man was Paul McAlpine, her landlord for the next three months.

Hoping desperately that her weak smile showed nothing of her chagrin, she said, 'I didn't know you were Gerard's cousin.' She tried to sound mildly amused, but each word emerged tinged with her discomfiture.

'Whereas I,' he said, 'had a pretty good idea that the Jacinta I met in Fiji and Gerard's Jacinta had to be the same person. He mentioned your height and was rather poetic about your hair. It didn't seem likely there'd be two of you about.'

He was the most handsome man she'd ever seen in her life, the impact of his strong, regular features emphasised by his startling colouring. Not many men of his age had hair the warm ash blond of childhood, so close to gold, and blue eyes without a trace of green or grey, and those who did were usually afflicted with pale brows and lashes that made them look pallid and juiceless. Paul McAlpine's were a brown so dark they were almost black.

On that hot, enchanted Fijian atoll he'd smiled—a smile

both utterly compelling and completely trustworthy. It had been almost too good to be true, that smile.

No sign of it now. The chiselled mouth was straight and the narrowed eyes aloof.

Jacinta's face set. Gerard's Jacinta? He'd merely repeated her sentence construction; of course he wasn't implying that she and Gerard had some sort of relationship. Nevertheless she felt she should make it very clear that Gerard was simply a good friend.

Before she could do that, Gerard's cousin said smoothly, 'Unfortunately there's been a hitch in plans. You can't stay in the bach because penguins have moved in.'

Wondering whether she'd heard correctly, she stared at him. 'Sorry,' she said inanely, wishing her brain hadn't fogged up. *'Penguins?'*

'Little blue penguins are quite common around the coast. Normally they nest in caves, but sometimes they find a convenient building and nest under the floors.'

Surely he couldn't be serious? One glance at those eyes—so cool they were almost cold, limpid and unshadowed—told her he was.

'I see,' she said numbly. Until that moment she hadn't realised how much she wanted to get away from Auckland. A kind of desperation sharpened her voice. 'Can't they be removed?'

'They have young.'

Something about his glance bothered her, and she stopped chewing her bottom lip.

He added, 'And they're protected.'

'Oh, then I suppose... No, they can't be disturbed.'

'They make gruesome noises when they return to their den at night—like a demented donkey being slaughtered. They also smell of decaying fish.' He met her suspicious glance with unwavering self-possession. 'Would you like to go and smell them?' he asked.

Unable to think of a sensible reply, Jacinta shook her head.

'You'd better come inside,' Paul McAlpine said.

Within seconds Jacinta found herself walking down a wide hall and into a beautifully decorated sitting room. Windows opening out onto an expansive roofed terrace looked over a lush lawn bordered with flowers and shrubs, with glimpses of the sea through sentinel pohutukawa trees.

Jacinta thought fiercely, I am not going back to town.

It would be like returning to prison.

And where had that thought come from?

'Sit down and I'll get you some tea,' Paul McAlpine said with remote courtesy, and went through another door.

Reluctantly Jacinta lowered herself into a very comfortable armchair and contemplated her legs, almost as ungraceful as her too-thin arms. Why on earth had she chosen to wear trousers of such a depressing shade of brown?

Because they were the best she had and she couldn't afford new ones. What did it matter? She didn't care what he or anybody else thought, she told herself sturdily, and knew that she lied.

'Tea'll be ready soon,' Paul McAlpine said, startling her with his swift reappearance.

Averting her eyes from his broad shoulders, and the way his well-cut trousers hugged muscular thighs, Jacinta swallowed. She even thought she could smell the elusive male fragrance that still infiltrated the occasional dream.

With a shock strong enough to be physical, she braved the icy brilliance of his eyes.

'Don't look so tragic, Jacinta. I have a suggestion to make.' There was a faint, barely discernible undertone to the words, a hint of cynical amusement that startled her.

Especially as she hadn't realised she was looking tragic. Taken aback, certainly, but 'tragic' was altogether overstating the case. Her hackles rose as he sat in the chair opposite her, so completely, uncompromisingly self-sufficient that her spine stiffened and she angled her chin in mute resistance.

Jacinta had no illusions about her looks; she knew that her height and thinness and the clearly defined, high-bridged nose that dominated her face were not redeemed by thick, violently ginger hair, or green eyes hazed with gold and set beneath straight, dark copper brows. Accustomed to feeling out of place amongst the chic women she saw everywhere, she was nevertheless outraged that Paul McAlpine should make her feel the same.

'Yes?' she said, aware that she sounded curt but unable to alter the tone to her usual confidence.

'I have several spare bedrooms,' Paul McAlpine told her. 'You're more than welcome to use one. My house-keeper lives in a flat at the back, so you won't be alone in the house with me.'

No sarcasm sharpened that beautiful voice, nothing even obliquely hostile glimmered in those blue eyes, but the skin pulled tight on the nape of Jacinta's neck as a shiver of cold foreboding slithered the length of her spine.

'That's very kind of you,' she said warily, 'but I don't think—'

He smiled. It was a smile that had probably stunned more women than she'd had showers. Silenced by its impact, she had to swallow when her words dried on her tongue.

Calmly, almost blandly, he said, 'If you feel awkward about living here with me I'll stay in a flat I own in Auckland.'

'I can't drive you out of your house,' she said, feeling both irritated and awkward.

His dark brows inched inwards. 'I believe that you had to move out of your flat, and as Gerard's sold his apartment you can't go there. I spend quite a lot of time either travelling or in my flat in Auckland; a few extra nights there won't be much of a hardship.'

What would it be like to own several houses?

After one swift, circumspect glance Jacinta realised she didn't have a chance of changing his mind. Thoughts churned around her mind, to be promptly discarded. She didn't have enough money to stay in a motel or rent another flat; the main advantage of Paul McAlpine's bach had been that it was free of charge.

He watched her with eyes half hidden by his lashes, waiting with a sort of vigilant patience—the remorseless tenacity of a hunter—that intimidated her in a way she didn't understand.

For heaven's sake! She was letting the aftermath of one dance ten months ago scramble her brain entirely.

With enormous reluctance she finally said, 'Then— thank you. I'll try not to get in your way.'

'Gerard said you're starting on your thesis.'

'Did he?' she said non-committally. 'What about Christmas?' she asked. 'Will the penguins be out from under the bach by then?'

'It's unlikely.' An enquiring eyebrow lifted. 'Were you planning to stay in the bach over Christmas?'

This would be her first Christmas alone. Through the lump in her throat she said raggedly, 'Yes. My mother died only a week after we came back from Fiji.'

'I'm sorry,' he said quietly. 'That was hard for you.'

Looking away, she nodded, swallowed and went on, 'I never had the chance to thank you for your kindness to her in Fiji. You left the day before us, and I—'

'I wasn't kind,' he interrupted. 'I liked her very much, and admired her gallantry.'

'She liked you, too.' Jacinta paused to steady her wobbly voice. 'She really enjoyed talking to you. It made her holiday. She was so determined I shouldn't miss anything…'

Cynthia Lyttelton had insisted Jacinta use the facilities at the resort, pleading with her to swim, to sail, to go snorkelling. 'Then you can tell me all about it,' she'd said.

Because the resort staff had been kind and attentive to her mother, Jacinta had given in. When she'd returned, salt-slicked and excited, after her first snorkelling expedi-

tion, Cynthia had told her about this man who had joined
her beneath her sun-umbrella—handsome as Adonis, she'd
said, and funny, with a good, sharp brain.

Gently, he said now, 'She told me she didn't have long
to live. I gather she'd been ill for a long time, yet she was
completely without self-pity.'

'She had arthritis, but she died of cancer.' I will not cry,
she averred silently, clenching her jaw against the onset of
grief.

'I'm so sorry,' he repeated, and she knew he was.

So many people—considerate, well-meaning people—
had told her that her mother's death must have been a
blessed relief to them both. She'd understood that they
were giving her what sympathy they could, but although
often in great pain Cynthia had enjoyed life, and she hadn't
wanted to die.

And Jacinta still mourned her loss.

She nodded, and they sat without speaking for some
moments while she regained control of her emotions.

Eventually she looked up, to meet a gaze that rested on
her face with unsettling penetration. Instantly his lashes
covered his eyes, and when they swept up again there was
nothing but that vivid, unrevealing intensity of colour, hiding all emotion, all speculation. His sculptured mouth had
thinned to a straight, forceful line.

A firebrand plummeted to the pit of her stomach. Instinct, so deeply buried in her unconscious she'd never
known of its existence, stirred, flexed, and muttered a
warning.

What am I getting into? she thought.

Common sense, brisk and practical, told her she wasn't
getting into anything, because she wouldn't allow herself
to. Paul McAlpine might look like every woman's idea of
a dream hero, with his golden hair and athlete's body and
disturbing mouth, but she didn't have to worship at his
shrine if she didn't want to.

'I usually have a quiet Christmas,' he told her. 'Anyway,

it's almost two months before we have to think of that. Our tea's probably ready, but if you'd like to come with me now I'll show you where the bedrooms are and you can choose one.'

Stiffly she got to her feet and went with him in and out of five superbly furnished bedrooms, all with both double-hung and French windows leading onto the encircling verandah. Just like something from a glossy magazine.

Jacinta refused to be impressed. In the end she chose one with a view of the sea solely because it had a long, businesslike desk on one wall.

'This one doesn't have its own bathroom,' Paul told her, 'but there's one right next door.'

'It'll be super, thank you.' Outside, the verandah had been furnished with a lounger and several chairs. Below the wooden balustrade flowers frothed and rioted. The room was pleasantly cool, with a daybed in one corner and an elegant Victorian dressing table, less ornamented than most of its kind. 'It looks lovely,' Jacinta finished sincerely. 'Thank you.'

'It's nothing.'

The negligent disclaimer was delivered in a deep voice, its obscurely equivocal intonation setting her teeth on edge.

She was being paranoid.

Well, it was probably normal. Although earlier that year she'd endured an unpleasant experience with a man, eventually her suspicions regarding masculine intentions must fade. Unfortunately it wasn't going to be a speedy process. Even with Gerard, who couldn't have been nicer, she'd found herself searching for sinister motives.

And now she was doing it again. Possibly because Paul McAlpine was so—so—well, so gorgeous. Her nervousness didn't mean she sensed anything ulterior; it arose from her physical awareness of him, which was her problem, not his. Behind Paul McAlpine's air of calm, confident good humour was simply that—calm, confident good humour.

Any ordinary woman would be jittery and a bit overwhelmed when confronted by one of the favoured few, a golden man with everything, including a presence that automatically made him a man to be noticed.

Exhausted, and therefore easily influenced, she simply needed time and peace to catch up with herself again. And here, in this beautiful, peaceful place, she'd get them.

Especially if her host was going to be away a lot.

They were halfway down the hall on the way to the kitchen when he said, 'Gerard tells me he's doing research for another book. I thought he'd just finished one.'

'Yes, but he found out that an old rival of his is intending to move in on his territory so he thought he'd better get going on this one and pre-empt him. Even in the academic world things can get rough when it comes to ego and staking claims.'

'I see. Is he planning to spend all his leave in the archives?'

'I think so. It was organised in such a rush that I'm not too sure of his plans.'

One eyebrow arched in a manner that showed only too clearly what Paul McAlpine thought of that, but he said nothing more. As she accompanied him Jacinta thought acidly that it was impossible to imagine this man ever doing anything on impulse.

In the spacious, very modern kitchen he introduced her to his housekeeper, a large-boned, blue-jeaned woman in her late thirties called Fran Borthwick, who smiled at her and said, 'Welcome to Waitapu. The tea's ready. Where do you want it?'

'I'll take it into the conservatory,' Paul said serenely, lifting the tray.

Jacinta returned the housekeeper's smile and went with him.

The conservatory, a delicious Victorian folly, was

equipped with rattan furniture upholstered in muted stripes. Jungly tropical growth sprouted from splendid pots; in one a huge frangipani held up white and gold flowers, their sweet scent reminding Jacinta forcibly of the week she'd spent in Fiji.

'Would you like to pour?' Paul McAlpine invited, setting the tray on a table.

Jacinta's gaze lingered too long on his elegant, long-fingered hands—hands that promised great strength as well as sureness. Resenting the mindless response that shivered across her nerve-ends, she said, 'Yes, of course,' sat down and lifted the teapot.

He liked his tea without milk and unsugared. Spartan tastes, Jacinta thought as she poured, then set down his cup and saucer.

It was an oddly intimate little rite, one that seemed right for the old-fashioned house and teaset. Ruthlessly ignoring the niggling edge of tension that sawed at her composure, she drank her tea and made polite conversation, wondering as she listened to his even, regulated voice whether authority and imperturbable good humour was all there was to Paul McAlpine.

No, he wouldn't have reached the top of his profession without intelligence and, she suspected, ruthlessness.

No doubt with women, too. The lover Gerard had pointed out that day in Ponsonby was a woman so beautiful she'd dazzled. However she was not the woman who had been with Paul in Fiji.

Perhaps he was promiscuous. Was that what Gerard had been hinting at with his reference to broken hearts?

Her quick revulsion at the idea was a warning, as was her conviction that he was too fastidious for crude promiscuity. All she knew about him was that he'd been kind to her mother, he'd been jilted—and he'd had two lovers in ten months.

And he danced well.

When his cool voice broke into her memories she

jumped guiltily, and had to pull herself together to answer his question about her degree.

'I majored in history,' she said.

'Yes, of course. Gerard's speciality. That's where you met him, I suppose?'

It was impossible to accuse him of prying. He must, she thought—surely irrelevantly—be hell in a courtroom. Any witness would be lulled into a sense of security by that lazy, calm voice that expressed nothing more than interest.

But he must have heard the reservation in her voice when she replied, 'I—yes.'

Dark lashes almost hid his eyes. 'I believe he offered you bed and board in his apartment. That must have been very convenient.'

Tautly she responded, 'He realised that things were—difficult—where I was living, and very kindly told me about a flat a friend of his wanted looked after while she took up a scholarship in England.'

For a moment the classically shaped mouth straightened, but when she looked again it was relaxed, even curved in a slight smile. 'Flatmates can be trying, can't they.'

It was not a question. Trying to lift the flatness of her tone, she agreed, 'Oh, they certainly can.'

'It sounds as though you had the ones from hell.'

'He—one was not—not congenial.' She put her cup and saucer down, relieved when they arrived on the table without any betraying chinks.

Paul said nothing, and after an awkward moment she went on, 'Gerard found me in the university library one night and realised that I was having a bad time.'

'Ah,' Paul said smoothly, 'he's always found it difficult to cope with tears.'

She fastened down her indignation. 'I wasn't crying,' she told him firmly, and added, 'He's very kind.'

'I'm sure he is,' Paul said, his voice soothing, almost mesmeric. 'Why can't you stay in your flat over the holidays?'

'A friend of the woman who owns it has moved in.'

When Gerard came back in February he'd go into his new house, a house with a flat joined to it, and she'd have a home once more. There was no reason she shouldn't tell Paul McAlpine that, but she fenced the words behind her teeth.

'And now you're waiting for the results of your final exams. Getting your BA has been a long haul. I believe there was a gap between the first two years and the last?'

Had her mother told him that her arthritis had become so bad after her daughter's second year at university that Jacinta had to give up her studies and come home to take care of her? No, she'd been a very private woman, so it had to have been Gerard. Hoping he hadn't coaxed Paul to lend her the bach by implying that she was a deserving case, she said evenly, 'Yes, nine years.'

'What do you intend to do when you've done your Master's? Teach?'

She shook her head. 'I don't think I'd be very good at that.'

Judicially, he observed, 'I shouldn't think there's much call for history masters outside the halls of academe.'

Why was she so—so nervous about her plans, so secretive? Because she didn't yet know whether they were possible—and because she didn't like the prospect of appearing a fool. 'Probably not,' she agreed, feeling ineffectual and foolish.

Goaded by his measuring look, she added, 'Actually, the Master's degree is a promise I made to my mother.'

There, that would show him she wasn't just drifting.

'And you always keep your promises?'

'Yes.'

Without haste her unwilling host surveyed her face, his vivid blue gaze roaming the thick, now untidy mass of her hair, its damp curls clinging to the margins of her high forehead.

Heat burned through her skin. Straight copper brows

drawn over her long nose, she met his scrutiny with defiance, knowing that the golden specks in her eyes would be glittering against the green matrix.

Starry Eyes, her mother used to call her when she was a child.

She could read nothing in Paul's scrutiny beyond a cool assessment that prickled her skin and tightened her muscles in a primitive reflex, but when his glance moved to her wide, soft mouth she jutted her chin, fighting back a response in which anger and a forbidden excitement warred.

She didn't want this overwhelming physical attraction. It was something she'd never experienced before, and it was dangerous.

Paul's enigmatic gaze didn't drop any further—and that, she thought angrily, was just as well. Although his scrutiny was too impersonal to be a leer, he'd checked her out beyond the bounds of politeness.

'''Mine honour is my life'',' he quoted.

Shakespeare, of course. An equivocal note in his voice scratched at her nerves again. 'Something like that,' she said curtly.

Each word dropped into the tense silence that stretched between them—humming, she thought edgily, with unspoken thoughts, with emotions she didn't intend to examine.

Just when she thought she was going to have to break it, he drawled, 'Very worthy.'

'Hardly.' She wondered why his words should sound like a warning. 'Every child learns the importance of keeping promises.'

'But children often forget as they grow older.'

Too late Jacinta remembered Aura, who had broken her vows to him in the most dramatic way. She opened her mouth to say something—anything—then closed it again when a covert glance at his shuttered expression warned her that nothing she could say would help ease the tension.

He asked her about the new fee structure at the university, and while they discussed the implications Jacinta forgot her reservations, forgot that almost insolent survey of her face. His astute, acerbic sagacity made her think hard and fast, and his understanding of people's motives startled her with its blend of tolerance and cynicism.

'Gerard seems to think you'll get honours when you do your MA,' he said, the blue eyes indolent behind his lashes.

Some obscure note in his voice made the comment ambiguous. 'He's a bit prejudiced,' she said stiffly. She might be Paul's guest, but she didn't owe him any more revelations.

'We're always inclined to be prejudiced about the people we're fond of,' Paul McAlpine said.

She looked sharply up, but those eyes, so transparent she could drown in them, hid his thoughts very effectively.

'Or those people we've taught,' she returned, just as pleasantly. 'I'll unpack now. Shall I take the tray through to the kitchen?'

'I will,' he said, getting to his feet and lifting the tray.

Although Jacinta always noticed hands, it was uncanny that the sight of his sent a tiny shudder of sensation chasing down her spine. Walking back along the hall, she felt an odd weight in her breasts, a kind of tingling fullness that embarrassed and irritated her.

Oh, be sensible, she told herself with self-derisory crispness, trying to be blasé and objective. It was hardly *surprising* that she should be attracted to him. He was magnificent—a splendid figure of a man. There was something about him that made her think of sanity and freedom and enviable, disciplined self-assurance.

Paul McAlpine would probably never find himself in a situation he couldn't control.

Lucky man, she decided crossly, blinking as she stepped from the shaded verandah into the bright light of the sun.

CHAPTER TWO

EVERYTHING Jacinta owned except for some stored furniture was contained in two suitcases. In the back seat of Gerard's car, neatly strapped in by the seatbelts, were a computer and printer, and on the floor several boxes of books.

Not a lot for almost thirty years, she thought wryly as she began to ease a suitcase out of the boot.

'I'll take that,' Paul said from behind.

Jacinta didn't quite stop herself from flinching, but hoped that her swift step away hid her involuntary reaction. 'Oh—thanks,' she said vaguely.

The sun gleamed on his fair hair, gilded his tanned skin. When he picked up the second case in one steady lift, muscles flexed smoothly beneath the fine cotton of his shirt. Oddly breathless, Jacinta reached into the back seat, fumbling with the seatbelt that held the computer in place.

A seagull laughed mockingly, its wings catching the light so that it shone silver, a mythical bow in the sparkling sky. Jacinta hauled the computer out and set off with it after the man who walked so easily up the white path and into the cool shadow of the house.

He put the suitcases onto the floor of the room she'd chosen and said, 'I'll bring in the printer.'

'It's all right,' she said. 'I can do it; you must have work to do.'

'Not today,' he said gravely.

Frankly helpless, she stood in the centre of the room with the computer in her arms and watched him go. Oh, lord, she thought dismally, walking across to the desk. Biting her lip, she turned and settled the computer into place on the desk.

He looked like a white knight, handsome and easygoing, a golden man—if you could ignore that strong jaw and the hint of hardness in his chiselled mouth. But from behind he looked like a Viking, walking with steady, long-legged, distance-eating strides across a world that trembled before him.

And although imagination was a prime requisite for her next venture, at that moment she wished she didn't possess quite so much of it.

He brought the printer in, and watched while she set it up. She did that because there was no way she'd open her suitcases in front of him. As it was, she was beginning to think that agreeing to stay here had not been a good decision.

While the test pattern ran through she said tentatively, 'I think we should discuss some sort of—of arrangement while I'm here.'

Those intimidating brows lifted again. He didn't say anything.

Jacinta imagined rods of steel going from her head to her heels. 'Money,' she said succinctly.

Eyes the same colour as a winter sky, cold and clear and piercing, moved from the screen to her face. 'You are Gerard's guest,' he said, his voice as unyielding as his expression. 'He asked me to make sure that you were all right while you were here. Money doesn't enter into it.'

She tried again. 'Nevertheless I'll pay for my food.'

He shrugged, his unreadable gaze never leaving her face. 'If it's that important to you, work out some sort of board payment with Fran,' he said negligently. 'As for anything else, just treat this as your home.'

She frowned. 'I don't want to intrude.'

'Oh, you won't,' he said quite gently, and smiled.

God! That smile was as uncompromisingly explosive as

Semtex. Jacinta had to draw in a deep, shaken breath before she could even think. Fortunately the printer whirred and chirruped, letting her know it was ready for work. Turning, she stared blindly at it, swallowed, and said, 'Thank you.'

'That looks very like Gerard's set-up,' Paul observed, his voice almost bland.

'It was,' she said shortly. 'When he got a new one he gave me this. They're obsolete as soon as you buy them, unfortunately. Not worth anything.' And she stopped because she'd started to babble, to explain, and she'd made a solemn vow that she was never going to do that again. The experience with Mark Stevens had cured her of ever justifying her actions to any man.

No man was ever again going to believe that he had the right to question what she did or what she thought.

Ever!

One brow drifted upwards. 'Aren't they? Not even as trade-ins?' Paul suggested evenly, and went out across the verandah into the sunlight.

Jacinta glowered after him. Did he think she was sponging off Gerard? Well, she didn't care! Not even if he did look like something chivalrous from a medieval tapestry, she thought sardonically, opening the wardrobe door and surveying the cavernous depths.

First of all she'd unpack, and then she'd go for a short walk—no, first she'd go and see the housekeeper and establish some ground rules.

She was almost in the hall when she realised that Paul was on his way back again, this time carrying a cardboard carton.

'From the weight of this I assume it's books,' he said.

Nodding, Jacinta firmly directed her gaze away as he set the box down on the floor. 'Thank you,' she said.

'I'll get the others.'

She knew how heavy those boxes were; Gerard had

helped her carry each one out to the car. Yet the weight didn't seem to affect Paul at all.

Jacinta looked with respect at his shoulders and said again, 'Thank you.'

'It was nothing,' he said, and left her, to reappear before she'd opened the first carton.

Once all the boxes were inside, he showed her the door to the bathroom and said, 'Make yourself at home,' before opening a door that presumably led into his bedroom.

Jacinta stood for a moment staring after him, her stomach gripped by some strong sensation. Hunger, she thought. You didn't have any lunch.

On the floor of the front passenger seat there should have been another carton, packed full of food. She'd brought everything in her pantry, supplementing it with groceries and perishables in the small town twenty minutes away, the town where she'd also taken out a temporary membership in the local library.

It wasn't there.

So Paul must have delivered it to the kitchen. Sure enough, when she'd made her way there, she saw the carton on the bench.

'Oh, he did bring it in here,' she said.

Busy kneading bread, Fran Borthwick smiled. 'Yes.'

'Tell me where to put everything.'

After the housekeeper had done that, and the food was stacked away in a well-stocked pantry, Jacinta explained that she wanted to contribute something to the housekeeping exchequer.

'Have you talked this over with Paul?' Fran asked, sounding surprised.

'Yes.' Jacinta repeated what he'd said.

Pulling off a chunk of dough, the older woman kneaded it expertly into a loaf and placed it into a baking tin. She said, 'Well, you pay whatever you feel is right. As far as meals go, breakfast's at seven. If that's too early—'

'No, no, that's fine,' Jacinta told her hastily.

'OK. Lunch at midday, afternoon tea at four, and dinner at seven-thirty.'

'When P—Mr McAlpine isn't here I'll get my own meals,' Jacinta said.

Fran gave her an approving glance. 'Good. There's always salads and stuff like that in the fridge.'

Back in the bedroom, fortified by a salad sandwich and a banana, Jacinta unpacked her suitcases and set out her books along the back of the desk. Then, obscurely comforted by her familiar things, she changed into shorts and a light shirt and slathered herself in sunscreen. With a wide-brimmed straw hat crammed over her ginger curls, she set off to explore.

About three acres of garden dreamed around the house, sheltered by the hedge on all sides except the seaward one. Even the salt winds couldn't get directly at it; pohutukawa trees leaned over both lawn and sand, forming a wide, informal barrier that would save Paul McAlpine from the indignity of having stray yachties peer into his house.

Seen between the swooping branches and dark, silver-backed leaves, the bay glittered, as blue as his eyes and as compellingly beautiful.

Jacinta wandered across the lawn and found a flight of steps that led out onto the sand, already sizzling under the hot November sun. Some people, she thought, remembering with a shudder the grim little house in which she'd spent most of the past nine years, had all the luck.

She didn't regret giving up her studies to care for her mother. In spite of everything there had been laughter and joy in that farm cottage. Still, she couldn't help thinking wistfully that her mother's long, pain-racked purgatory would have been more bearable in a place like this.

Fishing a handkerchief from her pocket, she blew her nose. The last thing she wanted was for Cynthia Lyttelton to be still enduring that monstrous, unbearable agony and complete loss of autonomy, but her death had left an enormous gap.

For years Jacinta had made all the decisions, done all the worrying. Grief, and relief that it was all over, and guilt about that relief, and exhaustion, had formed a particularly potent cocktail, one that had rendered her too lethargic to realise that Mark Stevens had begun a campaign to control her life.

Picking up a stone, she straightened and skipped it across the water.

Looking back, her slowness to understand the situation still astonished her. It had taken her three months to realise what was happening and leave the flat.

Another stone followed the first across the water.

With Gerard's help she'd got through that with very little trauma, and doing his housework three days a week had helped her save enough money to see her through the summer holidays without working.

All in all it had been a hard year; she was probably still not wholly recovered from her mother's death, but the crying jags were over, and the stress of trying to find some sort of balance, some firm place to stand, had gone. She'd come a long way in the last six months.

Oh, there were still problems, still decisions to be made. She had to work out what sort of life she wanted, and of course there was always money...

But for the moment she didn't have to worry about any of that. She had another promise to her mother to fulfil, and three months in this perfect place to do it.

Lifting her face and half closing her eyes, she smiled into the sun. Light danced off her lashes, the film of moisture there separating the rays so that they gleamed like diamonds.

Living in the bach would have been perfect. She'd probably only have seen Paul once or twice in the three months, instead of finding herself practically cheek by jowl with him.

Still, she'd manage. She was much stronger than she'd been before, much better able to look after herself. And it didn't really matter that she lusted a bit after Paul McAlpine. So, no doubt, did plenty of women. At least she recognised what she felt as straightforward physical hunger and didn't mistake it for anything more important.

The ringing of small, melodious bells filled the air. Jacinta stopped, watching and remembering. Outside the window of the cottage where she'd lived with her mother was a cherry tree, and each spring her mother had waited for the tuis to come and glut themselves on the nectar.

Just ahead, beside a transparent veil of water that ran over the sand, stood a clump of flax bushes. Strappy leaves supported tall stems with bronze- and wine-coloured flowers, mere tubular twists of petals with dark stamens protruding from the tip.

Yet in those flowers glistened nectar, and a tui, white feathers bobbling at its throat, sat on the stem and sang his spring carillon.

When Paul said her name Jacinta yelped, whirling to say angrily, 'Don't do that, for heaven's sake!'

Paul frowned. 'Your nerves must be shot to pieces.'

'No! I just wasn't— I didn't—'

'It's all right,' he said, his voice deep and sure and strangely soothing.

As the tui broke off its song to indulge in a cacophony of snorts and wheezes, interspersed with the sound of a contented pig, Paul put a hand on her shoulder, grounding her until the sudden surge of panic died away to be replaced by a slow combination of emotions—keen pleasure, and peace, and an oblique foreboding.

Swiftly she stepped away. 'Unusual birds you have here,' she said, snatching at her composure. 'Penguins that bray like donkeys, tuis that mimic pigs…'

'That's normal for both of them. Is it normal for you to jump like that whenever anyone comes up behind you?'

'No, but I didn't hear you and I suppose I am a bit tense. I thought that by now I'd be nicely ensconced in a bach with just the sea for company. Instead, I've been hijacked.'

She smiled tentatively and his frown disappeared, although his gaze was still keenly perceptive as it rested on her face. 'Where is the bach, by the way?'

Dropping his hand, he nodded to where a road left the main one and ran over the headland to the south. 'In the next bay,' he said.

She nodded too, not quite knowing what to say. The tui forgot its barnyard imitations and went back to foraging for nectar. Jacinta enjoyed the iridescent sheen of its plumage as the thin stem swayed in the sunlight—greens and purples, blues and bronzes, brighter by far than oil on water.

Every sense she possessed was at full stretch, so that she heard with keen pleasure the susurration of the waves on the beach, felt the heat and the wind on her tender skin, inhaled salty air and tasted her own emotions in her mouth, a sharp delight edged with wariness.

Paul didn't seem in a hurry to leave, so they watched the bird until Jacinta was unnerved enough by the silence to ask, 'What's the name of this bay?'

'Homestead Bay.'

She laughed a little. 'Of course. What a glorious place to grow up in.'

'I'm sure it would be,' he said calmly, 'but I've only owned it for five years or so.'

A note in his voice steered her well away from that topic. Too late she remembered that he'd bought it after he'd been jilted by the lovely Aura. Stumbling slightly, she asked, 'Is that the Coromandel Peninsula on the skyline?'

'And Great Barrier Island.'

Gloating, her eyes dreamy, she murmured, 'It's so beautiful.'

'I think so,' he said smoothly.

Jacinta stiffened. However banal and ordinary his words, there always seemed to be a subtext, some oblique intonation or cool, fleeting amusement adding an extra meaning to what he said.

She couldn't help but feel that in some subtle way Paul McAlpine neither liked nor trusted her.

And that was ridiculous, because she didn't know the man well enough to interpret either his tone of voice or expression. As well, he was a lawyer, trained to keep his features under control.

Although she was prepared to bet that they'd never been exactly open and candid. There was too much self-discipline in that beautiful mouth, and in spite of their vivid colour his blue eyes were surprisingly opaque, hiding Paul McAlpine's emotions very well.

She said abruptly, 'Gerard said you're a lawyer.'

'Most of my work is in international law,' he told her, a hint of reserve flattening his tone.

So he didn't want to talk about it. Neither had Gerard. 'Very high-powered,' he'd said. 'He deals with governments.'

Whatever that meant. As Paul's career seemed to be off-limits, she said, 'And is this a working farm?'

'Certainly. It's a stud; we breed Blonde d'Aquitaines, French beef cattle. We'd better go for a short tour to orient you.'

That not-quite-lazy, assured smile sizzled from the top of her head down to her toes, curling them involuntarily in her sandals. He knew very well the effect he had on women.

She returned his smile, pleased by the slight narrowing of his eyes as she said courteously, 'A good idea. I don't want to end up in the bull paddock.'

'Our bulls are normally placid enough,' he said. 'However, it is a good idea to keep away from them. Any large animal can turn dangerous.'

Like the man who owned them, she thought, startled by the insight. Ignoring a mental image of that easy self-reliance transformed by violent emotion into something much darker and infinitely more hazardous, she asked dulcetly, 'Do you think that pastoral farming has any future in a world that appears to be going green and vegetarian?'

A slight lift of one dark brow recognised the provocation in her question, but he gave a reasoned, restrained reply. This man would scorn an emotional response, an argument based on anything but facts.

Legal training again.

Another thought slipped so stealthily into her mind that it had taken possession before she realised its existence. Had he been hurt by his emotions, hurt so badly that he no longer indulged them?

Not that he looked like someone too wounded by love to risk it again, she thought after a snatched glance at the strong, clear-cut profile. Still, she suspected that his pleasant, approachable attitude was armour. She didn't know what lay beneath it, but she'd be prepared to bet that it would take intense goading to penetrate his shield of self-contained authority.

Gerard, who seemed to still have a mild case of hero-worship for his older cousin, had once told her that Paul never lost his temper.

Not even when Aura had told him she was going to marry his best friend?

As they walked past woolsheds, and an implement shed where brightly coloured monsters lurked, and beneath darkly needled macrocarpa trees along a fenced, metalled race that led to other paddocks, they talked objectively, intelligently, about the world and where it was possibly headed.

Jacinta filed little snippets of information away like hiding treasure. Paul McAlpine moved with a tightly leashed vitality that was at odds with his indolent appearance. He looked at each topic of conversation from both sides; he had a sharp, incisive mind; he enjoyed discussing issues, but when the conversation became personal he blocked.

He needn't worry, she thought when at last they came

back to the house. She'd be as detached and dispassionate as he was.

But these next three months would have been a lot simpler if those penguins hadn't decided to take up residence beneath the bach...

If only she had the money to say thanks, but no thanks, and walk away.

Unfortunately, her mother's legacy covered only her tuition fees—although since their rise 'covered' was hardly the word, and if they rose again next year she'd be in trouble. Her student's allowance paid the rent and bought her soap and shampoo and other necessities.

And she was being silly, letting Paul get to her.

She'd certainly make sure she paid her way here. Even if she did look and feel like an unsophisticated hick, she thought ironically as they turned back, she had her pride.

Inside the cool house, Paul said pleasantly, 'Dinner is at seven-thirty. If you'd like a drink first I'll be in the conservatory around seven.'

'Thank you,' she said non-committally, giddily aware of herself, of the way her long limbs moved, of the way her hips swayed, and the fact that her hair had once more slipped free of its clip and was clinging to her hot cheeks.

Back in her bedroom, she switched on the computer, opened a file, typed 'CHAPTER ONE', and then hesitated, before picking up a very old dictionary of quotations she'd bought for fifty cents in a garage sale. She found the lines quickly, from Shakespeare's *Richard the Second*.

Mine honour is my life; both grow in one
Take honour from me, and my life is done.

A hard creed, she thought; a creed for a strong man who held to a spartan belief.

Thoughtfully she closed the book, sat down in front of the computer screen and began to write.

At first the words came easily. She'd told the story so many times to her mother that she almost knew it by heart. *The unicorn snorted, its blue eyes shimmering in the moonlight*, she wrote. *'Very well then,' it said smugly. 'Don't blame me when the Master realises what you've done. I did my best to stop you.'*

But after she'd typed a page she stopped and read it, frowning. It looked—clumsy. And whenever she tried to summon the unicorn's image, its blue eyes had a disconcerting trick of changing to other eyes—quite different ones, cool and distant and enigmatic.

She got to her feet and glowered out of the window. The garden looked very desirable, the lounger eminently appealing.

Doggedly, Jacinta sat down at the desk again. She had promised her mother she'd write this and she was going to do it, even if it did look raw and childish and unformed on paper.

An hour later she got up and walked across to the French windows, trying to recall the look in Paul McAlpine's eyes when she'd told him that the computer equipment had been Gerard's.

Perhaps, she decided, trying to be fair, he had reason to worry about his cousin. She knew and Gerard knew that she wasn't trying to sponge off him, but to an outsider it could look that way. He'd lent her his car, would have lent her money if she hadn't refused it, and out of the kindness of his heart had organised this chance to fulfil one of the promises she'd made to her mother. He didn't know anything about the other promise she'd made, the one she was actually working on now. She owed him a lot.

And, talking of the car, she'd better see where she could garage it, because salt winds were notorious for causing rust. But before she bearded the lion in whatever den he was ensconced she'd go for a quick walk to the gate and back.

Out in the garden she smiled and clipped a leaf from

the lemon verbena. Her mother had loved its citrus perfume, sharp and delightful, and always had a bush of it in
the garden. And now she was dead, but the world was still
beautiful beyond belief, and it was an insult to her not to
enjoy it.

Blinking, Jacinta unlatched the gate and walked through
it straight into a pair of hard, masculine arms.

For a moment she thought she'd managed to stumble
into Paul McAlpine's grip, but the voice that said, 'Oh,
sorry, I didn't know you were there,' was younger than
his and lighter, the New Zealand drawl more pronounced.

'No,' she said, stepping backwards, 'I'm sorry, I wasn't
looking…'

Dark eyes rested on her face with unmistakable appreciation, and the smile he gave her was open and guileless
and very infectious.

'Dean Latrobe,' he said. 'I'm Paul's farm manager.'

Jacinta returned his smile and told him her name, adding
after a short pause, 'I'm staying here.'

'Oh, yes, the lady who's supposed to be spending the
summer in the bach,' he said, and grinned again. 'Paul was
ropable when I told him no one would last a night there.'

'I imagine he would have been,' she said, laughing a
little. 'But he very kindly offered me a bed for the holidays
just the same.'

'If you've got the keys,' he said, 'I'll put your car in
the garage. It is your car, isn't it?'

She said hastily, 'No, it belongs to Paul's cousin. He's
in America at the moment.'

'Yeah, thought I recognised it.' He ran a knowledgable
glance over it. 'He was up a month or so ago. Got the
keys?'

'I'll get them from my room,' she said. 'But there's no
need for you to put it away—if you'll just show me where
the garage is…'

'All right,' he said obligingly.

Jacinta hesitated. 'I'd better ask Paul first.'

'Why? There's room in the garage. Trust me, he won't throw his cousin's car out.'

Well, no, he hadn't thrown his cousin's protégée out, but that didn't mean he wanted her there.

'He's a hard man,' Dean Latrobe said cheerfully, 'but he's not unreasonable.'

In other words she was being silly.

'Trust me,' Dean Latrobe said, and winked at her.

He was nice, and there were no undercurrents in his smile or his voice. She laughed back at him and turned to go through the gate.

And there was Paul, the magnificent framework of his face clamped in aloof austerity, eyes slightly narrowed as they went from her smiling face to his manager's.

Startled, Jacinta stopped. 'I thought I should put the car away,' she blurted. 'Is that all right?'

'Yes, of course.'

'I just have to get the keys.'

Courteously he stood aside. Again absurdly self-conscious, she walked swiftly past him and up onto the verandah, found the keys in her bag and ran lightly back.

To find that Dean had gone.

Paul's vivid eyes dwelt on her face with a chilling lack of emotion.

Her smile probably flickered, but she said easily, 'If you'll point me in the direction of the garage, I'll put the car away.'

But Paul said calmly, 'I'll come with you,' and opened the car door for her.

Slowly she climbed in and waited. Because it gave her something to do, she wound the window down and made little fanning motions with one hand, saying as he lowered himself lithely beside her, 'This car really heats up in the sun.'

'Do you use it often?'

Recalled to herself, Jacinta hastily set the engine going and put the car in motion. 'Not often,' she said aloofly.

Once a week to pick up groceries from the supermarket, in fact.

'Turn left,' Paul said.

The drive ducked under an archway of Cape honeysuckle and over a cattlestop into a large gravel courtyard at the back of the house. A garage, doors open, formed one wing.

When the house had been first built, the other wing had probably been workshops and the laundry; possibly the pots of flowers at a door indicated a conversion to the housekeeper's flat. Between the two wings stretched the rear wall of the house. In the centre of the courtyard a well-planted herb garden surrounded an arbour where a glorious apricot rose bloomed with prodigal lavishness.

Jacinta concentrated hard on getting the car into the garage, braking with relief as the car slid to a stop beside a substantial continental saloon.

'You drive well,' Paul commented as she unfastened her seatbelt.

'Thank you.' She quelled a sharp pleasure.

'No wonder Gerard trusts you with it.'

'He made sure I could drive properly first,' she said, getting out and putting an end to the conversation as she shut the door a little too heavily.

Walking beside him to the back door, she wondered what on earth was happening to her. Nothing, she thought in profound irritation. She was simply overreacting to a man who attracted her very much on a physical level.

Clearly he felt no such attraction, which was just as well.

It might be more sensible to go back to Auckland and work over the holidays, but why should she run away? She could cope; this inconvenient awareness would die soon, and she'd promised her mother she'd write this book before the year was over, which left her only two months.

One day, Jacinta thought, she was going to earn enough money to give her some control over her life.

'I should perhaps mention that Dean is engaged,' Paul said evenly.

It took her a moment to realise what he was getting at, and when she did her first instinct was to laugh. For heaven's sake, what did he think she was—some sort of *femme fatale*, dangerously attractive to men?

That first response was followed by anger. Far more likely that he thought she was so desperate for a man that she'd flirt with anyone!

'That's nice,' she said agreeably, just managing to keep the note of mockery from her voice.

His swift glance scorched across her profile, bringing her senses to full alert as his mouth curled in a tight parody of a smile that revealed a glimpse of white teeth.

'Very nice,' he said, his voice suspiciously bland. 'Her name is Brenda and she teaches maths at the local high school.'

The colours of the garden sang in violent juxtaposition, and as Jacinta's eyes met his, half-hidden by his lashes, the blue gleaming like the sun on ice, she took a quick, impeded breath.

Beneath that unhurried, confident surface was a primitive streak a mile wide, and she'd do well to stay away from it. This man was every bit as fiercely predatory as a lion.

'Is she local?' she asked, because it was easier, less threatening, to speak than to stay silent.

His smile faded, and she was left shaken, wondering if she had been stupidly romantic when she'd compared him to a lion.

'She's the daughter of one of the oldest families in the district,' he said serenely.

A lion, for heaven's sake! How hackneyed.

Paul McAlpine was no more or less than a clever man, blessed—or cursed—with the sort of good looks and personality that made him automatically attractive to most women. The premonition, the icy breath of danger that had struck through her, was sheer imagination.

All right, she found him intensely attractive, and, yes, that was a nuisance, but it could be dealt with. It would pass, as such things do when ignored.

He held the back door open and Jacinta went through ahead of him, welcoming the room's cool refuge from the heat and the blinding light outside.

'I'll see you at seven,' he said.

It was an unequivocal dismissal, and although she'd been about to say exactly the same words, they stung.

With her shoulders very erect, she went down the hall and into her bedroom.

CHAPTER THREE

ONCE there, Jacinta didn't immediately go back to the computer. Slowly she walked across the room to stop in front of the dressing table and frown into a mirror burnished by that generous, silvery gleam that comes with age.

Perhaps that was why she looked different. Her mouth was fuller, redder, and the green in her eyes was highlighted by golden speckles. Even her skin had some colour in it—a tawny flush that brightened its usual pallor.

'Oh, grow up!' she said crossly, loudly, and turned her back on her reflection and went across to the desk.

Making up the story had been comparatively simple; she and her mother shared a love of fantasy literature, and one day, when Cynthia had been racked with pain and unable to read, Jacinta had tried to take her mind off her agony by soliciting her help with a story she'd had wandering through her mind for weeks.

Her mother had enjoyed the experience so much she'd insisted on an instalment each day, eventually asking Jacinta to write a book from the notes she'd made.

But what had seemed satisfying and complete when she told it was now a chain of words with no interest, no resonance, words that sat flatly on the page and produced no vivid images.

Jacinta was frowning at the screen when Paul McAlpine's voice jerked her head upright. He was outside, speaking to someone in the garden, and although she couldn't discern his words she could hear that he was amused.

And she realised what was wrong with her manuscript. When she'd told the stories to her mother the tone of her voice had provided colour and shading, drama and humour, despair and desperation. She'd have to use words to do the job.

'Thank you, Paul,' she said softly.

So absorbed did she become that when she next looked at her watch it was ten minutes to seven. Hastily she saved, backed up and shut the machine down, then gathered her sponge bag, towel and orange cotton wrap and went down the hall to the bathroom.

After another quick shower she dried herself, pulled her wrap on and hurried back to her room. She was almost at her door when hairs prickled along the back of her neck. Instinctively she flashed a swift glance over her shoulder.

Paul was standing in the door of his bedroom. Jacinta's pulse suddenly hammered in her throat as she registered the impact of his scrutiny right through to the marrow of her bones. He didn't say anything, but she could see dark colour along his cheekbones that both excited and astonished her.

'I won't be long,' she croaked, opening the door and sliding through it as fast as she could.

All right, she commanded her thudding, skipping heart, stop that right this minute! You're just going through delayed adolescence, that's all. You'll get over it.

And probably any man would be interested in a woman—however thin—who was walking about with nothing on underneath her worn cotton dressing gown. That was the way this sex thing worked; it certainly didn't mean that he wanted Jacinta Lyttelton, just that his hormones had been activated.

The wrap unpeeled from her damp body, she got into her bra and pants, then looked through her clothes.

Of course she didn't have anything to wear for a pre-dinner drink with a high-powered international lawyer who lived on a dream farm beside the sea. Something floaty and silken would have done, or casually chic resort wear, but she owned nothing like that.

Her hand hovered over a neat, fitting blouse of vivid orange silk and her teeth sank into her bottom lip. It was her only impulse buy of the past ten years, and she'd not even have considered it if her mother hadn't been with her in that small, spice-scented shop in Fiji, urging her to forget for once their cramped budget.

She'd never worn it, although the hot, bright colour magically transformed her hair and skin and the tight, short-sleeved underblouse and flowing skirt lent her body a grace she didn't really possess, especially when she draped the floating silk veil over the ensemble. The sari was fancy dress, calling far too much attention to its wearer.

Still, she thought, her eyes feasting hungrily on the intense hues, when she could afford clothes again, she'd choose those colours and to hell with basic black!

In the end it came down to a couple of skirts, both of which she'd made several years ago. Shrugging, she got into one, a plain rusty cotton that came to just below her knees. Over the top she wore a tee-shirt the exact green of her eyes, a lucky second-hand bargain from an op shop.

As though it mattered! Paul certainly wouldn't care what she wore.

Dragging her hair from its clip, she brushed it back from her face and folded it into a low knot at the nape of her neck. It was too thick and curly to stay there, but it would look neat enough for an hour or so.

At ten past seven she finally made her way down to the conservatory, despising herself for having to stiffen her knees before she went in.

When he saw her Paul stood up with an automatic courtesy. Although he was only a couple of inches above six feet, no more than four inches taller than she was, he seemed to tower over her as he said pleasantly, 'Good evening. What would you like to drink?'

No sign at all of any extra colour in his face, she told herself. See, it meant nothing.

'Soda water, thanks,' she said, sheer force of character preventing her from running the tip of her tongue over her lips. Parched as though she'd been lost in sand dunes for a week, she swallowed to ease her arid throat.

He wore a short-sleeved shirt which had almost certainly been made for him, and casual trousers that hugged his hips and revealed the musculature of his thighs. He looked like something from a smart men's magazine, except that he was far more—more *solid*, she thought, groping for the right word. Formidable, that was it. When you looked at Paul McAlpine you knew he was a man to be reckoned with.

He didn't press her to try something alcoholic, for which she was devoutly thankful because she felt drunk enough already. How unfair that she'd plunged into a full-scale crush! At sixteen such situations were accepted, treated with amused sympathy, even taken for granted; blushes and fluttering hearts and starry eyes were almost *de rigueur* while you were growing up.

At twenty-nine you ran the risk of making a total and complete fool of yourself.

She accepted the long, cold glass of soda water with its neat little circle of lime on top, green-skinned and comforting. Bubbles of moisture pearled down the sides as she lifted it gratefully to her lips and drank.

And hiccupped.

Paul gave a sudden grin. 'I always do that,' he said. 'It makes me feel about eight again.'

That smile should be banned.

Returning it as best she could, Jacinta said, 'I should stick to unfizzy drinks.'

'It would be a pity to miss out on champagne,' he said, pouring himself a weak whisky and soda.

'I've never tasted it,' she confessed. The minute the words left her mouth she wanted to recall them. They made her sound so unsophisticated, so deprived, and she was neither.

He didn't look surprised. That irritated her too. Perhaps he thought she lurked in the background of life like a Victorian poor relation, too spineless to do anything but be grateful for crumbs.

Meeting the enigmatic eyes with a slightly lifted chin, she squelched the urge to explain.

'Don't look so defensive,' he advised odiously. 'Plenty of people don't drink.'

Oh, he knew how to get under her skin. She showed her teeth and said, 'I'm not a teetotaller—I like cider and white wine. It just so happens that I've never tried champagne.'

'Not even on your twenty-first birthday?'

'Not even then,' she said. She'd done her shift in a takeaway shop that night, and her mother had cooked a special supper when at last she'd come home.

'In that case,' Paul said calmly, 'we should have some tonight. Sit down while I get a bottle.'

'No—I don't want—' Jacinta stared angrily after him as he strode out of the room; her irritation was very real, but even so her eyes lingered on his wide shoulders.

How smoothly he walked, silently, with a free, lithe grace that melted her bones.

God, she was beginning to be obsessed by him.

After draining half the glass of soda water without a pause or a hiccup, she went to stand at the window.

Almost immediately the colours and contrasts, the quiet hush of the sea and the darkening blue of the sky combined to drag her mind away from the crossfire of recriminations, so that by the time Paul came back she'd regained enough control to turn and say with a composed smile, 'This is very kind of you.'

'It runs in the family,' he said, a thread of irony lacing the comment as he put the bottle down on the drinks tray.

He eased the cork off, startling her into exclaiming, 'I thought it was supposed to pop!'

'Not if it's done correctly and hasn't been shaken,' he said, pouring the honey-gold liquid into two long flutes. Tiny bubbles ran up the glass to burst with subdued enthusiasm on the surface.

After a pause so slight she almost didn't recognise it, he picked up the glass and proffered it. She took it carefully, concentrating on the glass so that she wasn't looking into his face when their fingers touched and a tingle of electricity sizzled from that brief meeting of skin to some guarded, hitherto inviolate part of her.

Sizzles and tingles are all signs of a crush, she told herself cynically. Perhaps you should enjoy it.

'Congratulations on turning twenty-one,' Paul said, his voice revealing nothing.

'Thank you.' Lifting her gaze, she gave him a set, swift smile before lowering her lashes and cautiously tasting the delicious, frivolous contents of her glass.

It made her hiccup too.

'Oh, dear,' she said, the cool, wonderful taste prickling through her mouth. 'I suppose that's an insult to it.'

'Not if we both do it,' he said, sounding a thousand miles away.

She risked another rapid glance. He *was* a thousand miles away; the moment of communion had passed, and although he was smiling, and his voice was still level and amused, the blue eyes were guarded and remote.

Hurt—so stupid!—she took another sip of champagne and said, 'It's definitely worth waiting for. Thank you.'

With experienced skill he changed the subject, beginning with polite pleasantries that led within a few minutes to a vigorous discussion—so vigorous it almost became an argument—about a political issue. Jacinta enjoyed herself enormously, feeling her mind stretch under his probing, appreciating the keen satisfaction of measuring herself against such intelligence.

Formidable described him exactly.

And very composed; he argued with a singular lack of emotion that had her at a disadvantage several times. Some time later, setting out to refute a statement he'd made, she realised that her cheeks were hot and her voice was rising.

'Hey,' she said, breaking off her impassioned discourse to stare at her now empty glass, 'I'm talking too much. I think I'm drunk!'

'Hardly,' he drawled.

Jacinta put the glass down and pressed the backs of her fingers against her cheeks, hiding the flush. 'If I'm not, I'm getting there,' she said.

He laughed quietly. 'Dinner will fix that. Come on, Fran's just nodded through the door.'

Desperate not to stumble, she got gingerly to her feet, relieved to find that although her head swam a little she didn't sprawl across the floor or lurch into the furniture. Perhaps all it took to control her habitual clumsiness was champagne? She couldn't control a giggle at such an exquisitely amusing idea.

'That's a pretty laugh,' Paul said, holding the door open for her.

Still smiling, she explained, regretting it the instant the words left her mouth, especially when he looked her over thoughtfully. Alcohol and awareness were a powerful combination, releasing too many inhibitions.

'You're not clumsy,' he said as they went through another door. 'You move freely and easily.'

Well, what else could he say?

'You wait until I trip,' she said, hiding her stunned pleasure at the compliment with a tone of dark promise. 'I do it at the worst times.'

'In that case it sounds like self-consciousness, not clumsiness. And the only cure for that is developing some inner esteem.'

'A comment like that,' she parried, startled by his perceptiveness, 'sounds very New-Agey and unlawyerish to me.'

He laughed, but responded with energy, setting the subject for their conversation over dinner. They ate in a room set up as a living and dining area; it opened out onto a wide terrace overlooking the sea and the garden, so that the sound of the waves formed a gentle background.

And Paul was right; after the first course her head cleared completely, but she refused a second glass of champagne, asking anxiously, 'It won't go to waste, will it?'

And could have kicked herself. After all, half a bottle of champagne probably didn't represent any great loss to him.

'No,' he said. 'I have a special stopper that saves the wine from the air and keeps the bubbles in.'

She nodded, and perhaps some of the bubbles were still bursting softly in her bloodstream because she said, 'My mother was very keen on the "waste not, want not" bit.'

'So was mine,' he said. 'I think their generation was encouraged to be thrifty.'

'Unlike ours?'

His brow lifted. 'I don't make generalisations,' he said, teasing her about her inclination to do just that.

Jacinta grinned back. 'I don't make many.'

'Even one is too many.'

He was sitting back in his chair, looking down at the flowers in the middle of the table—satiny golden roses in a translucent white bowl. A long, tanned hand lay loosely on the table in front of him.

He looked, Jacinta thought, profoundly distant, as though the shutters had come down. There was no longer any warmth in his smile; it was merely a movement of his hard mouth, and his eyes were opaque, unreadable. He'd gone away and left her, and she felt cold and isolated and bereft.

'But that,' he said levelly, 'is what the lawyer in me says.'

And again, without seeming to, he changed the subject, leaving Jacinta feeling empty and unsatisfied, as though she'd been promised something and then arbitrarily denied it.

Later that night, wondering whether a walk along the beach would cure her restlessness, she stood in the dense shade of the pohutukawa trees and listened to the silence. It should have soothed her, sent her serenely to bed, but the steady drumbeat of her heart, the measured, inexorable pulse of excitement through her body, was too insistent to be denied. She stood on the edge of something perilous, something that might colour her life in the hues of summer—or fling her into wintry despair.

The moon, a slender curl in the western sky, silvered the crests of the small waves crisping onto the shore. Its magical light illuminated something else too: Paul McAlpine's head as he walked along the sand.

Jacinta's foolish heart jumped. He was moving slowly, hands in pockets, head slightly bent, and for the few seconds she watched him she thought she saw a vulnerability that wasn't there any other time.

Then he looked up and said in that textured, beautiful voice, 'I didn't realise you were there. Come down and join me.'

Embarrassed, as though she'd been deliberately spying on him, she jumped clumsily onto the sand, landing in its soft depths with an awkwardness that dumped her onto her backside.

Paul held out his hand, asking curtly, 'Are you all right?'

Oh, why had she told him that she tripped at the most inappropriate times? Would that astute mind pick up on her helpless attraction?

Oddly angry, she ignored his offer of support and scrambled to her feet. 'Yes, fine, thanks,' she said, dusting her hands free of sand. 'I forgot that the sand is always deep and dry at the top of the beach. At least it's easy to land on. And I did warn you that I tend to trip over my feet a lot. You might think it's lack of self-esteem but I've always done it, so it's more likely to be a combination of long legs and a bad sense of balance.'

'You could be right,' he said negligently. 'Can't you sleep?'

After two hours of work on the manuscript she was wired, too strung up to even think of going to bed. At least, that was her excuse—she refused to even consider that talking to Paul over the dinner table had affected her so powerfully.

Hoping she didn't sound evasive, she murmured, 'It's such a gorgeous night.'

His smile was a swift, white flash in the darkness. 'Yes. This place seems to specialise in glamorous nights. You'll have to enjoy it without me tomorrow as I'm staying in town.'

'Auckland must be a jolt to the system after Waitapu,' she said prosaically, suppressing a glimmer of nameless emotion.

His shoulders moved in a slight shrug. 'Oh, it has its pleasures.'

The woman in Ponsonby, she thought swiftly, painfully.

He continued, 'I used to live there until I bought Waitapu. While I'm away I'd like you to check with Fran if you decide to further your acquaintance with the property, and of course always tell her where you're going and when you expect to be back.'

Although everything inside her rebelled at the calm suggestion, she nodded. He was right; the last thing his nice farm manager would want was some idiot wandering around getting herself into trouble.

'I'll do that,' she said. 'I don't plan to stray too far from the homestead, but I'm used to living on a farm so I know the protocol.'

'Were you brought up on one?'

'No, we lived in a little one-horse town,' she said. 'We moved to Auckland when I was eighteen so I could go to university. Then my mother was confined to her wheelchair and she longed for the country, so we moved back to a farm cottage on the outskirts of another small town.'

'In Northland?'

'No. A village on the Hauraki Plains.'

It had been a tiny cottage, with two small bedrooms and a big room that was living room, dining room and kitchen. The fence huddled near the house, enclosing a rank, overgrown lawn that the farmer's wife had mown the day they moved in. But it was all on one level, so that as her mother's disease progressed she could get out in her wheelchair, and while she was able she and Jacinta had turned the lawn into a cottage garden, growing their own vegetables and producing flowers from seeds and cuttings and divisions given to them.

Jacinta's eyes blurred as she wondered what had happened to that garden, her mother's last and most loved interest.

'And are you like your mother? Do you prefer living in the country?' Paul asked with idle interest.

Unconsciously she shook her head. 'I don't know—yes, I suppose I do. But I enjoy Auckland.'

'What, particularly?'

'I've loved university, and I like the cultural things— the art galleries especially. And although it's not politically correct, I like Auckland's brashness, that feeling that anything's possible, that the world is a playground and we should all be enjoying it.'

They had reached the end of the beach; he stopped and looked at the low headland crowned with old, sprawling, comfortable pohutukawas. 'That casual attitude would be a lot harder to maintain without the climate and the gulf. New Zealand's other main cities simply don't have the weather to be brash and casual.'

One day, Jacinta told herself, she'd be as familiar with those cities as he so clearly was. Excitement, frothy as the waves, bubbling like champagne, filled her, threatening to reveal itself in her face. Beneath the headland, wave-smoothed rocks rose through the sand; on the pretext of examining one, she moved away.

She could have walked beside him in the beguiling splendour of the moonlight for hours.

Just talking. That would be enough.

But because she understood that soon it wouldn't be enough, she couldn't allow herself to do this again.

The weather, she told herself. Keep talking about the weather; its very banality would temper her emotions.

'We do have a great climate,' she said, 'although some of the students from the south find the humidity unbearable in summer.'

Yes, that was the right touch. Her voice sounded cool and uninvolved, the conversational tone implying that this was not important stuff.

That he was not important.

And how could he be? She didn't know him.

'Ah, Auckland's proverbial steam bath,' he said, an ironic note underpinning the words so that she wondered whether he knew what she was doing. 'You get used to it.'

'You can get used to anything, they say.' Jacinta fervently hoped that this was true.

They walked back along the beach towards the silent house, the light from its windows gleaming through the swooping branches of the trees.

They talked of art and music and their favourite rock bands and sport, only falling to silence as they came up the steps to the lawn. With noiseless footsteps they crossed the grass, dew-damp already, its scent mingling with the soft salt fragrance of the sea.

All Jacinta's responses—to the night-perfumed air, the dim shadows and blurred forms of flowers and foliage, the luminous, light-embossed sky—were heightened by the man who walked beside her. Unbidden anticipation lodged in the pit of her stomach, honed her senses to a keen, subliminal edge.

Four steps up, the verandah surrounded three sides of the house. Beneath its roof lurked a pool of darkness, a still, breathless haven between garden and rooms. Because Jacinta wanted nothing more than to stay outside with Paul, where she wasn't reminded that this man had everything and she had nothing, she took the steps too quickly.

And, of course, she tripped.

Before she had time to fall, hard hands grabbed her by the hips, jerking her back. For fleeting seconds she was held against his strong body, and for the first time in her life she understood the meaning of hunger.

'Thanks,' she muttered, wrenching herself away as though his touch scalded her. Fighting back the urge to scuttle for the safety of her bedroom, she stopped halfway across the wooden boards, grateful for the darkness there.

The words she'd intended to say died. Paul hadn't moved, and beneath his lashes his narrowed eyes gleamed. With eyes attuned to the starlight Jacinta could even see the tiny flicker of a muscle along his jawline.

Her bones deliquesced. She'd barely had time to think exultantly, He feels it too! when he reimposed control and the moment's betrayal was wiped from features now mask-like in their rigidity.

In a voice that revealed only a studied aloofness, he said, 'You'd better watch that step.'

Watch *your* step, he meant.

Swallowing to ease the dryness in her mouth and throat, Jacinta said, 'I will. I did warn you,' adding rapidly, 'although I usually fall down steps, not up them.'

She couldn't bear it if he thought she'd done it deliberately, as a self-seeking, trashy little ploy to attract him.

This was not simple sexual attraction. Whatever it was, it had the power to bring her to total meltdown. How long had she spent in his arms—a couple of seconds? Two seconds to change a life, she thought feverishly.

Terrified by the wild, blind hunger that savaged her, she retreated a pace towards her bedroom. Her sandals made little scuffing noises, barely audible over the pounding discord of her senses.

'There's the phone,' Paul said. 'Excuse me.'

Inwardly shaking, her eyes dilated and wary, she gazed after him. Breathe, she ordered; just breathe slowly and calmly, and this panic will go away. But before she could summon wits enough to walk into her room, he was back.

'It's Gerard,' he said laconically, expression and voice giving nothing away. 'He wants to say hello.'

'Oh, yes,' she said, stumbling over each word as she skirted him with ridiculous care.

When she picked up the receiver Paul walked out of the room, and she stared at his receding back, saying with an odd, unbidden nervousness, 'Hello, Gerard.'

'Paul said you're staying at the homestead. With him,' Gerard said, his voice unexpectedly close.

'Yes.' Dismayed caution iced her tone. She knew he meant nothing by it, but she refused to make excuses. Frowning, she said levelly, 'Penguins are nesting under the bach.'

There was a moment's silence. Jacinta was about to ask, Are you there? when he said, 'I see. A real nuisance. How are you getting on with the notes for your thesis?'

'I haven't done anything yet,' she said, guiltily resentful of his well-meant interference.

In his generous way, and certainly without realising it, he was trying to force her along the path he'd chosen, dismissing her occasional objections with a tolerant persistence as though she were a small child who needed guidance.

Mark had been sure she needed guidance too.

With a flash of sardonic humour she thought it was strange that although she'd been running her life for years now, in the short space of a year two men had decided she needed their instruction and direction. Perhaps she was giving off vibrations? If so, they were lying ones.

She'd make all her own decisions.

'I see.' Gerard's voice cooled. 'I'd thought I might do some research for you while I'm here.'

'Gerard, I haven't even decided what subject I'm tackling, so it would be wasted effort,' she said, knowing there was no tactful way of saying it. Hastily she added, 'How are you finding Harvard?'

'Cold,' he said stiffly.

'Poor thing. I won't upset you by telling you it's glorious here.'

'No,' he said abstractedly, 'please don't do that.' Again there was a hesitation before he said, 'I hope Paul's being good to you.'

'He's very kind,' she said, her voice flattening.

'He's a decent man, the best. I wish he'd get married, but I don't think he'll ever recover from Aura's betrayal.'

Jacinta's heart clamped in her chest. 'He doesn't look like a modern equivalent of Miss Havisham,' she offered. She didn't want to hear this; with any luck the reference might divert the conversation.

'Who? Oh, Dickens. *Great Expectations.* An overrated writer, in my opinion. Well, Paul's certainly not training up a small child to wreak revenge on all members of the opposite sex, but I think when Aura jilted him it killed something in him. Since then he's had affairs, of course, but he doesn't like women much.'

Was that it? Was the reservation she'd sensed in Paul right from the start so impersonal, a simple mistrust of the whole female world?

Crisply she said, 'Well, that's none of our—'

'Aura was so beautiful,' Gerard interrupted mournfully, refusing to detour. 'The sort of woman you never forget. I don't know how she could do it.'

'It happens.' Jacinta knew she sounded flippant, but she

most emphatically didn't want to hear how wonderful the woman who had jilted Paul was.

'I suppose it does. Disloyalty is becoming more common than it used to be, I'm afraid.'

'Careful, Gerard,' she said lightly, 'your years are showing. I don't suppose it was easy for her, either. Decisions like that take some courage. Oh, there was a little rattle in the back of your car on the way up. Do you want me to take it into the garage?'

'No,' he said. 'I know what it is—nothing serious.' His voice altered. 'Well, I'd better go. Missing me?'

'I—yes—yes, of course,' she said, taken aback.

'Take care of yourself, and don't flirt with Paul. He might reciprocate, but he does with every woman he meets. It doesn't mean anything.'

'Flirting never does,' she said. 'That's the essence of the game, surely? To have fun and break no bones? Goodbye, Gerard. Do you want to speak to Paul again?'

'No,' he said. 'Goodbye, Jacinta.'

It was impossible to imagine Paul listening at the door, but as she hung up he came into the room. An eyebrow climbed and he said evenly, 'That didn't take long.'

Perhaps because she'd been discussing him, colour surged upwards from her breasts. 'He just wanted to see how things were going,' she said, carefully banishing the defensive note from her voice.

He nodded, his gaze very shrewd and hard as it rested on her face. 'Would you like a nightcap?'

'No, thanks; I'll go to bed now.'

He stepped aside to let her past. Almost stifled by his size and potent presence, Jacinta hurried through the door and down the hall to her bedroom, closing the door behind her with a shattering relief.

And then, with the curtains safely drawn and the light turned off, she sat in the darkness and shivered while those moments when Paul had held her stormed back into her brain, refusing to cede to any other thoughts.

It was nothing, she told herself. He supported you, that's all, until you got your balance back.

But her pulses were still throbbing through her body with a hypnotic rhythm, and when she closed her eyes she could see the arrogant, chiselled features outlined by the faint glow of the stars, and recall how his sheer, sexual power had consumed her.

Helpless, snared by her primitive, involuntary response, she'd been unable to move.

How could any woman leave him for another man? She simply couldn't believe it. Aura Whoever-she-was must have been a fool.

Jacinta drew a deep breath. It would pay her to remember that he'd retreated behind his armour of self-sufficiency with insulting speed. And it had been antagonism she'd glimpsed in his narrowed eyes.

If she sat here in the dark like a lovelorn teenager, going over and over how his arms had tightened like iron around her, how the heat of his body had enveloped her, she'd be pushing herself deeper and deeper into the murky waters of infatuation.

Setting her jaw, she got to her feet and switched on the light.

As she got ready for bed Gerard's words came back to haunt her. Did Paul dislike all women because one had let him down so spectacularly?

It didn't seem likely; surely he was too sane, too intelligent to generalise so brutally? But if he'd really loved that runaway fiancée the betrayal would have seemed hideous.

Disillusionment did strange things to people.

'Your problem,' she informed her reflection softly as she brushed the long, curling silk of her hair, 'is that you want whatever he feels for you—even if it's only dislike and mistrust—to belong to you alone, not to some unknown woman with more looks than nous.'

This fixation was becoming wretchedly inconvenient.

Ah, well, she'd be able to talk some sense into herself while he was away. Naturally she was a little off balance—she hadn't been expecting to find herself living in the same house as a man with such powerful, incendiary impact.

But as she lay in bed listening to the quiet sound of the sea through the trees, she let her mind drift, and soon became lost in a romantic daydream that merged imperceptibly with sleep, and turned erotic when the constraints of will and self-discipline blurred and vanished.

CHAPTER FOUR

JACINTA woke the next morning with heavy eyes, and a voluptuous exhaustion weighed her down. It was succeeded by a shocked scurry from the bed as memory replayed in vibrant colour the images she'd conjured up from some sensuous, uninhibited, completely unsuspected part of her psyche.

'Oh, lord,' she whispered, uncomfortable and tense as she turned the shower onto cold and stepped determinedly in, 'I've never had that sort of dream before!'

Flicking her hair out of the spray, she scrubbed herself with punishing vigour, and began stubbornly to plan the day's writing. When she finally emerged from her bedroom she'd regained some fragile measure of composure.

She was dressed for the morning in a thin white cotton shirt that hung loosely over her cinnamon three-quarter-length pants. For some inscrutable reason she'd succumbed to a feminine instinct and donned her one good pair of sandals, elderly though they were.

Although for all the glamour they added she might just as well have worn her cheap rubber sandals; they wouldn't have looked much more out of place against the muted opulence of the oriental runner that glowed on the wide, polished boards of the hall. The house was still cool, but it was going to be another unseasonably hot day.

Her hard-won composure fled when she walked into the breakfast room, for there, cup of coffee in front of him, sat Paul, dominant and uncompromisingly masculine, sunlight dancing around him in a golden aura.

'Good morning,' Jacinta said, reining in her reactions with a ruthless hand. 'No, don't get up, please.'

But he did, setting a sheaf of papers down on the table. 'Sleep well?' he enquired.

'Yes, thank you. I thought you'd be gone by now.' And she could have bitten her tongue, for she'd sounded surly and far too aware of him.

'In ten minutes,' he said. 'I gather you don't wake up in the best of moods.'

It was an excuse, but one she couldn't accept. 'Just this morning,' she said, trying to sound casually offhand. 'I think I must have slept too heavily.'

'A headache?' He seemed genuinely concerned.

'No,' she returned gruffly, 'a thick head and a bad temper.'

'Then help yourself to whatever you want,' he said, a note of amusement warming his voice, 'and I won't talk to you.'

His calm, confident good humour banished her surliness instantly. With a rueful smile she turned away to ladle fruit and cereal into a bowl.

If he stayed aloof she'd be all right. Times like this were going to be the problem; when he laughed he was altogether too likeable, the sort of man a woman could lose her heart to.

While he studied his papers Jacinta chewed cereal that tasted like cardboard, and tamarillos with no more flavour. She buttered toast. She drank coffee. Mentally she urged him to get up and leave.

Even though she kept her eyes studiously averted, she *felt* him. His beautifully tailored clothes made her cheap, second-hand ones look shabby and sleazy, and his self-possession was a blow directed at hers.

Finally he got to his feet and Jacinta was forced to look up. His eyes were so blue, she thought mindlessly.

'Enjoy yourself,' he said with laconic pleasantness. 'I'll

see you tomorrow night, although I won't be here for dinner.'

Ah, thank God, he'd retreated once more behind the armour of his pleasantness. 'Have a good day,' Jacinta returned, deliberately banal.

When he left it the room echoed with emptiness. She heard his car leave, and the house suddenly died. After forcing another cup of coffee down an unwilling throat, she cleared the table and helped Fran put the dishes away before walking down to the beach to watch the gulls slowly wheel overhead.

At length, obscurely soothed by the never-ending, remorseless ebb and flow of the waves, she returned to her bedroom, tidied it and made the bed, and sat herself down in front of Gerard's computer.

She'd wondered if her sexual reaction to Paul might inhibit her writing, but it was as though someone had pressed a hidden button and released a barrier in her, the excitement of her writing somehow seeming to join with the languor and the febrile passion that lingered like a miasma from her dreams.

For hours she wrote with complete concentration, ignoring the sounds of the farm around the house, until Fran tapped on her door and called, 'Jacinta, do you want some lunch?'

'Hang on,' she answered, and finished the paragraph she was working on.

'I'm sorry to interrupt,' the housekeeper said when she emerged, 'but Paul said to make sure you had meals.'

Jacinta came crashing back into real life. 'Oh,' she said. 'Oh, I didn't realise... I thought... Is it lunchtime already?'

'Past one o'clock. Your work must be going well.'

Jacinta nodded, realising that she was both hungry and a little stiff. 'Very well,' she said cheerfully. 'But I thought we'd agreed that I'd make my own meals when there's just us.'

Fran's look was dry and amused. 'In this house what

Paul says goes. He told me to see that you ate decent meals at the right times, so if you're not out in the kitchen making your meals, I will be.'

She should be angry; after all, she'd hated it when Mark had tried to manage her life, and she resented even Gerard's well-meant suggestions. It was a measure of her infatuation that she felt a tiny warm glow at Paul's thoughtfulness.

Bad response, she thought gloomily, heading towards the kitchen with Fran.

That day set the pattern for the one following—and the one after that, for Paul rang the housekeeper to say that he wouldn't be home that night either, and possibly not for another couple.

I am not disappointed, Jacinta told herself firmly when Fran relayed the news after putting a cup of peppermint tea on one of the verandah tables.

The housekeeper and she had come to an agreement. If Jacinta was typing Fran didn't interrupt, but left food and cups of various interesting drinks on the table outside the bedroom, which Jacinta ate and drank when she emerged.

No, Jacinta thought when the housekeeper had gone, I'm not in the *least* disappointed.

And she went on being not disappointed for the next two days, until she found herself gazing at the page number on the computer screen with something like awe. That was a lot of pages, especially since she was only a two-finger typist.

It was late in the afternoon, the drowsy, slightly ragged end of the day when the sky looked washed out and the earth longed for the refreshing arrival of dusk.

This November was shaping up to be the hottest she'd ever experienced—too hot and dry for farmers. Only the previous evening Dean had told her he was worried about the prospect of a drought. They'd met when she'd gone for a walk before dinner, after being chased from the kitchen by the competent Fran. Dean had stopped his four-wheeled farm bike, and they'd chatted.

He'd noticed her interested look at the quad and offered, 'I'll give you a go on it if you like.'

'With dogs or without?' she asked, eyeing the two black and white collies that perched on the back. 'I might tip it over and they'd get hurt.'

For answer he got off, whistled the dogs onto the grass, and Jacinta spent an enjoyable half hour while he showed her how to drive the bike.

'A natural,' he said eventually. 'I'll hop on the back and you can give me a ride to the homestead.'

Elated at her new accomplishment, Jacinta had done just that, finishing with a flourish in the courtyard outside the back door, laughing as Fran came out to see.

'Thank you,' she said, smiling up at Dean when he got down to help her off. 'I haven't had so much fun for ages!'

He turned to Fran. 'She's a born farm bike rider.'

'Rather her than me,' Fran said, smiling as her glance switched from his face to Jacinta's and back again. 'And you'd better start looking for a born rainmaker, if the long-range weather forecast is right.'

'Are we in for a drought?' Jacinta asked.

'If we don't get rain soon,' he said, squinting at the cloudless sky, 'we'll be in deep and serious trouble.'

But although Jacinta had sympathised, she was enjoying the heat.

Putting down the pages of her manuscript, she wandered out onto the verandah and picked up the mug of peppermint tea, pretending that she wasn't waiting for the sound of a car.

A glance at her watch revealed that it was only five o'clock. Even if Paul did decide to come home tonight he wouldn't be there until after six, unless he got off early.

With determination, she drank the peppermint tea and read the newspaper, then took the cup back to the kitchen.

'You look beat,' Fran said, coming in through the door

with a great handful of salad greens from the herb garden. 'As hot as me.'

'I am.' Jacinta washed and dried the mug, edgy and restless and unable to think of anything she wanted to do to fill in the time.

'Why don't you go for a swim?' Fran asked.

Jacinta asked suspiciously, 'How warm is the water?'

'By November it's as warm as it's ever going to be.'

'I suppose so.' She put the cup and saucer away and said, 'Actually, I'm a wimp about swimming. I have this fantasy that one day I'll be rich enough to afford a heated pool.'

'Join the club,' Fran said cheerfully. 'Paul swims most of the year.'

'Masochist.' But she wasn't surprised.

Back in her room, she unearthed the bathing suit she'd thrust into a bottom drawer. Although an old bikini, it hadn't been used much; while she'd looked after her mother she'd rarely had a chance to swim. Except for Fiji, of course, and then she'd stuck to early in the morning and late at night so that the sun wouldn't burn her skin. Paul hadn't seen her in it.

She got into it, pulled a tee-shirt over the top, and fossicked out a large towel adorned with a pattern of brightly coloured birds.

Fran was right. The water was seductively warm, so she swam for twenty minutes until, limbs languid and weighted with effort, she walked out of the sea, pulling her hair free from the old rubber cap that had kept it dry. It rioted around her head, the thick ginger curls lifting in the slight evening breeze.

At the sound of an engine she looked frantically around for her tee-shirt. But even as she set off towards the towel she heard Dean's voice and relaxed.

'Good swim?' he asked, eyeing her with frank, not unpleasant admiration.

She smiled. 'Wonderful. It's so warm—too warm. I feel as though I've swum a hundred miles.'

He pushed his hat onto the back of his head and grinned at her. 'It does that to you. The blue water's early,' he said. 'The big game sportsmen'll be catching marlin before long.'

'What's the blue water?'

'Oh, tropical currents. Usually it doesn't come inshore until after Christmas, but this year Davy Jones must have known you'd be here and sent it down early.'

Jacinta grinned up into his nice, unhandsome face. She liked Dean, and clearly he liked her; he'd told her all about Brenda, his fiancée, and that they planned to get married in a year's time, and although he looked at Jacinta with candid appreciation there was nothing more subtle in his eyes than a healthy male enjoyment.

When the fairy godmothers had handed out her basic qualities at birth, they'd forgotten to include sex appeal. Boys had liked her, but very few had asked her out. Her mother used to say it was because she was taller than most of them; Jacinta knew she simply didn't have that special quality that made men desperate.

Even Mark hadn't wanted her body; he'd wanted somebody to control, to dominate, someone who'd boost his fragile ego.

'I'd better go on up,' she said. 'It gets a bit chilly out of the water.'

She took a step, tripped, and saved herself with both her hands.

'Here,' Dean said, and hauled her upright. When she winced his grip tightened and he demanded, 'What happened? You all right?'

'I'm clumsy,' she said lightly, 'but I think I must have stood on a broken shell.' She bent her leg at the knee, twisting to peer down at the uplifted sole of her foot.

'It could have been glass. Let's see,' he said, dropping to a crouch beside her and taking her foot in his. 'No, it's not bleeding,' he informed her after a thorough inspection, 'but the skin's marked.'

His thumb rubbed across the sensitive sole, and she gurgled and said, 'You're tickling!'

'Sorry,' he said, laughing and looking up at her with teasing eyes.

The sound of a quiet, 'Good evening,' cut into their shared amusement with the biting, brutal accuracy of a scalpel. Jacinta flinched as though she'd been struck, jerking her foot free from Dean's grip.

He stood up, still smiling, and said, 'G'day, Paul.'

Paul was still in his suit; he should have looked incongruously formal there on the beach, his shiny black city shoes half sunk in the sand, his head smoothly brushed and gold in the sinking sun.

Instead he looked terrifying. And yet there was nothing about the handsome face, nothing about the regular features or the cool blue eyes to set Jacinta's heart thudding sickly, the adrenalin surging through every vein in a swift, warning flood.

Unless it was the splintering moment when his gaze raked the length of her scantily clad body before fixing on Dean's face.

She drew in a ragged breath.

Apparently unaware of anything out of the ordinary, Dean went on cheerfully, 'I need a word whenever you've got time.'

'How about now?' Paul didn't look at Jacinta.

'Yeah, fine.' Dean directed his uncomplicated grin at her. 'Catch you later.'

Jacinta watched them go up under the trees and walk across the lawn towards the back of the house. Slowly, carefully, she expelled the breath that had been imprisoned in her lungs, and bent to pick up the tee-shirt at her feet.

After pulling it on she went back to the house and washed the sand from her legs under the tap beside the back door. She sat down on the steps and dried her feet, then hung her towel over the clothesline and went back inside, intent on seeking sanctuary in her bedroom.

She had to make herself walk normally past the closed door of the office because her whole instinct was to tiptoe.

As she showered the salt from her body she tried very hard to convince herself that she hadn't sensed an over-whelming blast of antagonism from Paul. There was no reason for it, unless he thought that as an engaged man Dean should be a little more circumspect with women.

However, he hadn't seemed angry with Dean.

How long had he been there? He must have seen her trip.

Perhaps he thought she tripped whenever a man came near her. Humiliation oozed through her, but she banished its slimy residue. All right, so she did care what he thought of her.

She was too conscious of Paul, too nervous and tense when he was around, and she was sick of it. She should leave, but—oh, why not admit it?—she wanted to stay.

Her childish infatuation wasn't doing anyone any harm; it wasn't as though she was making a nuisance of herself. And if she got hurt—well, she'd be the only one to know.

She chose her most concealing dress—a short-sleeved thing in soft, tawny cotton that flowed easily—hoping it would wipe from his mind the memory of her body in the scanty bikini.

And she stayed in her room, reading through the day's work, until emerging as close to seven-thirty as she could without seeming to avoid Paul. Relieved to find the con-servatory empty, she walked out onto the terrace and crouched beside the pond with its resident flotilla of gold-fish—large, streamlined creatures of gold and bronze and an orange so intense it was like the heart of the sun.

They were interested in human company, these fish. 'Hello,' she said quietly, and they came swimming up, nosing the fingers she put in the water.

She laughed softly. 'No, I haven't got any food. Furthermore, Fran tells me you don't need to be fed.'

'Fran's right,' Paul said from behind, his deep voice toneless.

Jacinta leapt to her feet, turning a flushed, startled face to him. He'd come around the corner of the house, walking through the light of the westering sun.

'Hello,' she said, working hard at a casual smile.

'Fran tells *me* you've been working all hours,' he said, leaning against one of the pergola uprights. Wisteria blossom, white and purple and lilac, cast shadows on his angular features.

She nodded. 'It's coming along rather well,' she said cautiously.

'Are you actually making notes for a thesis?'

After a moment's hesitation she admitted, 'No. I'm fulfilling a promise I made to my mother before she died.'

He nodded, and because he didn't ask she explained, 'I didn't want to tell Gerard because I could well be just wasting my time.'

It sounded both lame and defensive, and she wished she'd kept quiet.

'I see,' Paul said, his voice cool and non-committal. 'Are you planning to go ahead with the Master's degree?'

She should certainly have kept quiet. 'I don't know,' she finally confessed, astounding herself. Taking her MA was the other promise she'd made to her mother, but for the first time she wondered whether she really wanted to do it. It made her feel disloyal and mean.

'What will you do if you decide to give it a miss?'

'I'll find something,' she said, irritated with him for probing.

What she'd like to do was continue writing, but she was a realist—she knew she was unlikely to get her manuscript published. Writing was a highly competitive field and she was a total novice. And even if she was good enough and lucky enough to be published, it could be years before she earned sufficient to be able to do it full-time.

His shaded face gave nothing away, whereas she was in the full glare of the sun; when she realised that she was staring at him she dropped her lashes and pretended to be very interested in the slowly cruising goldfish, feeling hot and foolish and gauche, and resenting both herself for responding so foolishly to him and him for conjuring up that response.

'It's not an enviable position to be in,' he said after a moment, his voice judicial.

She shrugged. 'I'll manage. Did you always know you were going to be a lawyer?'

His mouth twisted. 'I wanted to be an adventurer. At school—a very traditional boarding school—my best friend and I planned a life swashbuckling around the world, but my father was a solicitor who wanted me to follow in his footsteps. And as he was ill that's what I did.'

A promise to a dying parent was hard to break. Smiling, Jacinta asked, 'What happened to your friend? I suppose he turned into an accountant.'

Then she remembered what Gerard had told her about that best friend.

'Oh,' he answered with a chilling lack of emotion, 'he fulfilled his dream. He developed from a tough kid to a dangerous man, who eventually gave everything up to grow grapes and make wine.'

With Aura, the woman Paul had wanted—probably still wanted.

Jacinta said, 'And have you ever regretted making the decision to obey your father?'

His quiet laughter had a cynical note to it. 'No, my father knew me better than I did. I enjoy what I do, and in its less overtly dramatic way it has enough adventure in it for me.'

He moved out from beneath the wisteria, and she was

jolted once more by his sheer male beauty—the elemental golden glory of his colouring, the formation of the bones beneath his tanned skin that would ensure he made an extraordinarily handsome old man, the powerful male symmetry of wide shoulders and lean hips, long legs and muscled forearms—and by his personality that so totally overshadowed his looks.

Six inches shorter, she thought, with washed-out eyes and features like Quasimodo, and he'd still stand out in any crowd. That unforced authority—the indomitable mixture of intelligence and mastery and focus, of courage and endurance and resolution—rendered him unforgettable.

'You're fortunate in your profession,' she said unevenly, an unbidden excitement fanning a flame inside her.

'Very.'

When he came towards her she had to stop herself from stepping backwards, but her fleeing feet carried her sideways, and although she concentrated with ferocious intensity on not stumbling, her wretched sense of balance—or lack of it—let her down again. It wasn't a dramatic lurch, but he caught her arm.

'Careful, even if you do like the fish we don't want you joining them.'

'No,' she said, rendered witless by the touch of his hand. 'I've already had my swim for the day.'

'And enjoyed it, I gather.'

'Yes, it was super.'

Inside the room she moved away from him. When Dean had touched her she'd felt nothing, yet she'd shivered to the core of her being at the light pressure of Paul's hand on her arm.

'How's your foot?' he asked now, glancing down.

Trying to stop her toes from curling, she said, 'What?'

'Your foot.' The words were patient, as though he were speaking to a child. Or a halfwit. 'You cut it on the beach.'

'No,' she said, 'I just stood on a sharp shell, I think. When we had a look there was nothing there.'

'Good. Dean was worried in case there was glass on the beach, but it would have broken the skin. You're sure a thin sliver didn't work its way in?'

'Quite sure,' she said fervently.

'In that case, sit down and I'll get you something to drink.'

He chose chilled white wine, but didn't try to persuade her to have any with him, instead giving her the lime and soda she asked for.

There was, she thought as she accepted the cold glass, nothing even vaguely threatening in his attitude. She'd just imagined things down on the beach.

Aloud, she said, 'Did you have a good time in Auckland?'

'I actually flew to America,' he said, smiling at her astonishment. 'To Los Angeles.'

'I didn't know barristers went all around the world.'

'We go wherever we're needed. In this case, I had to organise a meeting with American lawyers to set up a deal for a film production company.' He told her a little about it—no mention of names, nothing she could use to identify any of the people—and made her laugh several times with his ruthless puncturing of a couple of enormous egos.

'Do you have much dealing with film producers?' she asked.

'Quite a lot. New Zealand's becoming very popular for both film and television companies from overseas now, and where there's money there are people determined to protect their investment.'

'It sounds very glamorous,' she said, looking out through the open French windows to the lawn. The late light was sifting down through the clouds of sunset, falling in thick rays across the lawn. Anticipation began to build in her, a slow, heady buzz that was so close to being physical she could almost feel it licking sensuously as fur across her skin.

'It can be.' His lashes fell, half concealing his eyes.

'Would you like to come to a party with me in a couple of days' time? It's a wrap-up for a television series that's just been made here.'

'Oh—no, thank you,' she said after a scant moment of frozen, yearning hesitation. 'It sounds very interesting, but—'

One dark eyebrow lifted and he asked disconcertingly, 'But what?'

Jacinta decided that the truth was the only way to go. 'I don't have the right clothes for it,' she said bluntly, considering the sari for a micro-second before discarding the idea. 'And I don't have the money to buy any new ones.'

'I'm sorry.' He transferred his glance to the glass in his hand, surveying the cool gold liquid with its hints of green.

If he offers to buy me something, she thought furiously, I'll— I'll—

But he went on tightly, 'That was crass of me.'

She didn't refute that. It had been crass—surprisingly so for a man whose courtesy seemed inbred. Pride kept her head high. Poverty was nothing to be ashamed of.

Setting her glass down, she said, 'I don't feel I can spend my mother's legacy on clothes I might never wear again.'

'Is what you wear so important?' he asked with apparent idleness.

She snorted inelegantly. 'Not many people are confident enough to feel good in clothes that don't fit the occasion,' she said, and only when she'd finished realised that she was probably talking to one.

'You're right, of course. I'm sorry you can't come with me; I think you'd have enjoyed it.'

He began to talk about the forthcoming election, and eagerly she followed suit, enjoying that keen, incisive brain until Fran appeared at the door and said, 'Dinner's ready.'

As she went with him into the morning room Jacinta

knew she'd never forget that Paul McAlpine had once asked her to go with him to a party.

After eating the superb dinner without actually tasting it, she went back to work in her room so that Paul didn't feel obliged to entertain her. She wanted too much to stay there and talk to him, and listen to that slow, deep voice, and watch that arrogantly handsome face, and feel little chills of awareness run through her like a summons to heaven.

However, running away didn't work.

She closed the curtains to prevent marauding huhu beetles and moths and mosquitoes from dive-bombing her, and sat in front of the computer and stared at the screen, summoning a variety of images, none of which had anything to do with writing.

Eventually she shook her head and switched off the machine before getting ready for bed. When she'd turned the light out, she opened the curtains again to let the sweet, salty air wash into the room.

Perhaps because she went so early to bed she didn't sleep well, waking with a jolt at one in the morning and spending the next hour tossing and turning and trying to blank out the pictures in her mind. Around two she got up and, thinking ironically that life in New Zealand would be a lot easier without the assorted insects that roamed the night, closed the curtains once more before sitting down to write.

An hour or so later a quiet tap on her door made her jump.

'Just a minute,' she called out, dragging on her dressing gown.

It was Paul, clad in shirt and trousers. 'Are you all right?' he asked, scanning her face with unhurried thoroughness.

She nodded. 'I'm fine. I just couldn't sleep so—am I disturbing you?'

'No,' he said abruptly. 'I couldn't sleep either, so I went

for a walk and saw your light on. I thought I'd better investigate.'

'Thank you for checking.' She hesitated, then said, 'Goodnight.'

'I'm going to make some tea,' he said. 'Do you want some? Or do you prefer cocoa at this hour of the night?'

She should say no. She should be firm and aloof and definite—but polite, of course. Instead she yielded to unbearable temptation. 'Tea will be perfect.'

'Would you like me to bring it here?'

'No.' The word came out far too fast and hard. Conscious of her hot cheeks, she said, 'I'll come along to the kitchen,' and stepped back.

He said, 'I'll see you soon,' and went off down the hallway, moving soundlessly.

Five minutes later, respectable in a tee-shirt and a pair of jeans, Jacinta padded quietly down the hall and into the kitchen.

As she came in Paul lifted the electric jug to pour the boiling water into a teapot. When the pot was filled he looked up and smiled.

You should have said no, Jacinta told herself—too late to be of any help. Oh, you should have said never, not at this hour of the night, not if you're going to smile at me...

'Were you working?' he asked.

'Yes.'

'What exactly *are* you doing on Gerard's computer?' He reached to get a couple of mugs down from the cupboard.

Unwillingly Jacinta's eyes followed the slow, purposeful coil and flexion of muscles, the smooth signs of latent energy that marked his every movement. A sweet pang of desire caught her by surprise, demolishing her defences.

She had to force herself to concentrate on what he was saying.

'Fran's dying to know, although she'll never ask—not even me. She's been dropping hints, however. And I must admit to considerable curiosity myself. If it's a secret don't tell me.'

'I think I'm writing a book,' Jacinta confessed, amazed at her surrender.

'Well, yes, I rather gathered that you were. What sort of book?'

Flushing, she said resolutely, 'My mother used to really like reading science fiction, but she found that a lot of it was too technical.'

'The hard stuff,' he said. 'She was a *Star Trek* fan, I'll bet.'

She laughed. 'Of course she was. And she loved the *Star Wars* trilogy too. When she got too sick to be able to read herself, I used to read to her. We got talking about one particular book, and I said that it was all wrong, the characters didn't fit the plot. So she challenged me to give them a plot that fitted them better, and I began to make up a story about a group of people in an alternative universe, where unicorns had always existed, along with dragons and the phoenix.'

She blinked a couple of times and steadied her voice. 'She loved it, and after a while she started to come up with ideas too, and we'd discuss how we could fit them into the book. It gave her something to think about, helped her get through some pretty bad times. When medication clouded her mind so that she began to forget incidents, she suggested I make notes.' Uneasy at the way he was watching her, his eyes remote and yet oddly sympathetic, she looked away briefly.

Gently, he asked, 'Is this another promise?'

'Yes.'

'Have you ever done any writing before?'

Jacinta shrugged. 'I told stories continually throughout my childhood to anyone who'd listen. And when I was an adolescent I wrote obsessively—all about death and destruction and myself. Very gloomy and self-centred.'

'I find that hard to believe,' he said, his eyes amused.

'Aren't all teenagers?'

'I don't recall being gloomy,' he said. 'Self-centred—
yes, I'll admit to that. But everyone's self-centred when
they're fifteen.'

'I certainly was,' she said with a grimace, wondering
just what he'd been like as an adolescent. Always confident, no doubt; that assurance was as much a part of him
as the colour of his hair and his brilliant eyes.

'So how is the manuscript getting on?'

'Slowly. It's the oddest thing. I know this story and
these people so well, yet I'm having real trouble getting it
right.'

'I imagine that in telling a story you use voice and ges-
ture and timing,' he said thoughtfully, reaching into the
fridge to get out the milk. 'You have to supply that with
words in writing.'

Secretly impressed, Jacinta said, 'That's it exactly. It's
far harder than I thought it would be, but I am enjoying
it.'

'Fran worries about the long hours.'

'Fran should have been a nanny,' Jacinta said, smiling.
'I told her not to bother getting me meals, but she keeps
knocking on my door and insisting I eat regularly. Which,
I believe, is your fault.'

'Do you want me to tell her to leave you alone?'

Rather shocked at his cool authority, she shook her
head. 'Oh, no, I like structure to my day. I like the food,
too.'

'In that case she can continue to knock,' he said dryly,
pouring the tea.

They drank it in the morning room. Jacinta chose an
armchair, very comfortable and slightly oversized, as everything in the house was. To go with the owner, no doubt.

Paul settled lithely onto the sofa, long legs straight in
front of him, broad shoulders against the back, the mug of
tea somehow not in the least incongruous in his hands.
Jacinta thought—before she realised where her mind was

taking her—that his masculine grace overcame the full impact of his size, preventing him from looking clumsy or hulking.

'Gerard certainly wouldn't approve of the use you're making of his computer,' he said thoughtfully, watching her from eyes that should have looked sleepily half closed, but instead revealed the quick, clever mind behind his handsome face.

The name jarred across her contentment. She said quietly, 'I do intend to work on several proposals for the subject of my thesis. I probably should be doing them now, but I don't want to stop writing.'

'I see,' he said, and that smile set her spine tingling. 'You're hooked!'

It was foolish to feel that he'd lightened a burden for her. 'That's it exactly,' she said. 'But Gerard wouldn't understand. His taste in light reading tends to be—'

'Heavy,' Paul supplied laconically. He was silent for several moments, then asked, 'Have you done any walking while you've been here?'

'Oh, yes.' She leaned forward eagerly. 'Dean took me over to the bach yesterday afternoon. How on earth are you going to get rid of that awful smell?'

'We'll dig it out and make sure there's no way they can burrow underneath again,' he said lazily, his lashes drooping.

She frowned. 'Where will the penguins nest then?'

'They've bred perfectly happily in the caves at the base of the headland for thousands of centuries; they're like humans, taking the easy way, the shortcut, whenever they can. I hear you've learned to ride the quad. Fran said you looked as though you'd been on one for years.'

She laughed and told him about it. 'It was great fun, and in the end even the dogs deigned to ride with me.'

'Then you must have impressed them with your skill.' Beneath his heavy lids his eyes gleamed, blue as the bluest sapphires. 'Did Dean tell you that he and Brenda intend to buy their own farm soon?'

'Yes.' And because Paul believed in helping hard work, he'd offered to finance them. Dean and Brenda spent most of their spare time with land agents. 'I think it's a wonderful idea, and very generous of you.'

He frowned. 'He told you a little too much,' he said curtly. 'What else have you been doing?'

There was a slight note of—sarcasm? cynicism?—in his voice. Jacinta drank some of the tea before saying, 'I went into town with Fran and changed my library books. Apart from that, not a lot.'

'Swimming, obviously. How's the water?'

'Lovely.' Hastily, before she could blush like a fifteen-year-old, she added, 'Like swimming in silk.'

'I must come with you tomorrow.'

Which brought even more vivid images to her mind, so vivid that she drank the tea down too quickly and excused herself as soon as she could without being rude.

CHAPTER FIVE

HALF an hour later, back in bed but too tense to sleep, Jacinta relived those words. Her stomach jumped the way it had when he'd said them, at the vision her reckless brain had produced of Paul in swimming togs.

He's not for you, she told herself sternly, turning over to find a cooler place in the sheets. Not for you at all. Just grit your teeth and endure this violent crush because eventually it'll wear out. They always do.

But, oh, how potent it was, this singing in the blood, this untamed hunger that prowled through her days and nights, constantly testing the bars of her will and common sense. Eventually, when the stars were paling in the dawn sky, she managed to drift off into a heavy, dreamless slumber.

Next morning when she sat down and read over what she'd written the day before, she realised that the hero of the book was becoming more and more like Paul McAlpine.

Gritting her teeth, she went through and changed him back into the man she'd originally imagined; if she let Paul infiltrate the pages the characters would be set wildly at odds, because the plot she and her mother had created depended entirely on the interplay of each personality.

And her hero needed nothing of Paul in him.

Well, perhaps a little, she thought, lifting her eyes from the screen to gaze out across the lawn, still wet from heavy dew. Below the verandah the apricot and pink spider flowers of a grevillea bobbed as a tui landed heavily in the bush and proceeded to plunder their nectar. Sunlight burned across iridescent feathers, bathing him in blue and green and purple fire against the crisp white pompom at his throat.

Yes, there were similarities between Paul and Mage; both were leaders of men, both possessed the authority that came from confidence and success. But Mage was a grimmer, more severe man, and he had a fatal flaw, one he had to overcome. He loved jealously, absolutely, utterly.

A far cry from Paul's serene self-assurance, Jacinta thought with a wry grimace.

Although if Gerard was right—if he'd loved Aura so much that he could never love another woman—that indicated an extravagance of passion very much at odds with the man Jacinta knew.

Moodily she wondered how the unknown Aura, that dark flame of a woman, had captured Paul's heart so completely. And what sort of person was she to leave him like that?

'None of your business,' she told herself robustly, and got back to work—using it, she realised with some shame, to block out her emotions. It seemed a cowardly way to cope with them, but at least she didn't spend all day longing for Paul to return from his office in Auckland, and she certainly finished a lot of pages.

When the sun dipped westwards anticipation began to condense within her, almost physical in its impact, until she was wound as tightly as a spring. In a pathetic attempt to ease it, she went for a walk along the beach, striding strongly while she pretended to be thinking of the next day's work, trying to ignore the need and excitement that strummed a fiery counterpoint inside her.

She'd turned beneath the headland and was walking back in the dense shade of the trees when she saw a tall figure on the beach. Stopping, she feasted her eyes in passionate, eager scrutiny of the sleekly muscled wedge of his torso gleaming above brief black trunks, his lithe grace as he strode across the sand. Like a god, she thought, gilded by the sun, a primeval figure of beauty and power and leadership.

Almost immediately he turned his head and stopped. The air between them sparkled and spun, danced with tension, formed a glittering chain that linked her to him like shackles, like a psychic union.

It lasted only a second. He waved and turned towards the sea. Her heart thudding, Jacinta waved back before fleeing through the garden to the back of the house.

'Aren't you going for a swim?' Fran asked, looking up from the herb bed. 'Paul's just left.'

'How about you?' To hide her face, Jacinta bent to pick a blue borage flower, the exact colour of Paul's eyes.

'Too busy,' Fran said briefly.

Jacinta stood up. 'I'll see you later,' she said vaguely, her pulses still jumping, her body throbbing.

She didn't have to swim. Oh, Fran might think it odd if she didn't—but why should she? Why should she think about you at all? Jacinta asked as she headed for her bedroom. Let's be honest. You're looking for excuses to share an experience with him. You want to swim in the same sea as he is, breath the same air, be warmed by the same sun.

Expectation scorched from nerve-end to nerve-end, hollowing her stomach, tightening her skin.

Closing her door behind her, she said aloud, 'All right then, do it, but at least accept what you're doing. And no more nonsense about quivering air and psychic links!'

Once in her bikini she hesitated for a moment, then pulled on a tee-shirt; she'd keep it on even when she was swimming. If anyone—if Paul—made any comment, she'd say she didn't want to burn.

When she came out onto the beach he was swimming strongly several hundred metres from shore. Her sensible half was relieved; the other—the secret half, the half that longed intolerably for him—was eaten by disappointment.

Briskly she strode into the water and struck out away from that gleaming dark gold head, trying to purge herself of the tides that washed through her so darkly, so inevitably, gathering momentum day by day.

Even though she was exhausted when she finally made her way back across the sand, the cure hadn't worked. She dragged in deep, shuddering breaths, raking a trembling hand through her hair as she pulled the old rubber cap off and shook her hair down past her shoulders.

Behind her, Paul was heading for land. Perhaps, she thought tiredly, he had demons to exorcise too.

Moving slowly, she scooped up her towel and wrapped it around her waist, then made her way through the cool shade of the trees, climbed the steps up the bank and set off across the lawn.

Vibrant whistling warned her that someone was coming from the gate; summoning a smile, she glanced up as Dean strode around the corner of the house.

He finished with a loud, clever variation of a wolf whistle, then as he got closer eyed her with some concern. 'You look as though you've been pushing it,' he commented. 'You're a bit pale.'

She made a comical face. 'I decided I was getting slack, sitting in front of a computer all day, so I swam too long.'

'No,' he said, grinning, 'not a sign of slackness.' His eyes moved and his grin widened as he said to the man coming up behind her, 'No sign of slackness in you, either.'

'I should hope not,' Paul said. He'd swum for longer than she had, but he wasn't even puffing.

As Jacinta turned she felt the casual grip of his hand on her shoulder, burning through the wet material of her tee-shirt, scorching her composure. Startled, her lips parted and she looked into his face.

He didn't return her puzzled glance. His eyes, cool and unyielding between his thick, wet lashes, were fixed on

Dean. 'Did you want to see me?' he asked, lifting his hand from Jacinta's far too responsive shoulder.

'I do,' Dean said, his voice oddly formal. 'We need to discuss a staffing problem.'

'I'll see you in the office in ten minutes,' Paul said. 'See if Fran will get us a drink, will you?'

'Sure,' Dean said, smiled at Jacinta with none of his usual cheerful cheek, and left them.

'Are you all right?' Paul asked calmly.

Jacinta nodded. 'Fine. I just went for too long, but I don't want to get unfit. And writing all day is not exactly exercise.'

His brief touch had altered some subtle balance or perception of power, leaving her confused and upset. Every sense was on full alert, avidly soaking in the subtle signs of his masculinity, the vivid, bottomless blue of his eyes, the way the sun gleamed over the burnished slide of wet, golden skin, the masculine pattern of hair scrolled across his chest then arrowing down his flat stomach to disappear beneath the black material of his trunks...

And through the sensory overload came the coldness on her shoulder where his hand had rested.

'I hope,' he said, a bite to his words, 'you don't swim like that when I'm not here.'

'I'm not stupid. I do know my own limitations.'

Thank heavens she was wearing her tee-shirt and her towel! His gaze was intent and utterly disturbing; if she'd had nothing on but her bikini she'd have been enormously embarrassed.

As it was she knew that her nipples were stiffly peaked by a combination of cold and the drag of bra and shirt. Automatically she folded her arms across them and stepped back.

'I hope you do,' he said, and suddenly there was that undercurrent, the note of warning she'd heard when she first arrived at the homestead. 'You're cold. Come on.'

To her astonishment he took her hand and set off for the back door.

Once Jacinta had woken from her dazed grief after her mother's death she'd objected very much to Mark's dominating tactics, but for several moments she went meekly enough with Paul, her pulse jumping under the grip of his long fingers until—almost too late—her instincts shouted a warning. Reflexively she jerked her hand back. His fingers tightened for a second, then he released her.

'Have a warm shower,' he said. 'You still look cold.'

'I'll wash the sand off my feet first.'

Keeping her eyes well averted, she tried to turn the outdoor tap on, but after a moment of her fumbling with it he said, 'Here, let me,' and moved her hand off.

As the water gushed out he straightened up, looked her over with a narrowed, metallic glance, and said, 'Don't stay in the water for so long next time.'

Safely in the bathroom she stared at herself, seeing a woman she didn't know, a woman whose eyes gleamed pure gold beneath sultry lashes, whose mouth was soft and cushioned as though it had just been kissed, whose normally sallow skin was warmed by the lingering delight of those seconds when his hand had closed around hers, strong and warm and safe.

A woman whose breasts strained against the clinging material of the tee-shirt, the nipples prominent and completely at the mercy of the powerful sensations that rushed through her, white-hot and quite unmistakable.

'What am I going to do?' Jacinta asked that unknown woman. 'What on earth am I going to do?'

Angrily she turned the shower to cold and got in under the spray, flinching as needles of water washed away the salt and the heat.

Unfortunately, cold though it was, the water was unable to quench the rising desire that ate into her composure.

For desire was what it was, not the innocent, unformed intensity of a crush; she wanted Paul McAlpine, wanted him so badly she ached with it, and she was perilously close to surrendering to that feverish desperation.

It was just as well he didn't show any signs of reciprocating, because if he did she could well make a complete and utter fool of herself.

Paul could have any woman he wanted; he wasn't likely to want a tall, thin woman entirely lacking in that mysterious quality called allure, because of course the woman who'd gazed with such lazy sensuousness from the mirror was a momentary aberration.

Jacinta wished she'd had more social life when she'd first gone to university eleven years before. Although several men had asked her out, she'd refused them because she'd needed to spend every spare moment working in a local takeaway bar.

But if she'd gone out with some of them she'd have gained some much-needed experience. She might have realised much sooner that Mark was developing an unhealthy attitude towards her, and, more importantly, she might now have some idea of how to deal with her own responses and emotions to a man so different from Mark.

However, she thought mordantly as she towelled herself dry with rather too much vigour, none of the nice men who'd asked her out then would have been able to teach her how to cope with this sudden, inexplicable hunger for a man she could never have.

At dinner that night she was very cool, very restrained, determined to stay aloof, but after half an hour of his pleasant, unthreatening conversation she relaxed, eventually feeling secure enough to watch a television programme with him—an excellent drama with a premise based on the overwhelming passion for each other of two violently disparate people.

When it was over she said, 'Romeo and Juliet I can understand—they were so young. But love at first sight is a hoary old chestnut.'

'One you don't believe in?' he asked, smiling faintly, his hooded gaze resting on her face.

'I certainly don't. Love needs time to grow. The two people in that play were obsessed with each other, but although it was dramatic and overwhelming it's not what I call love.'

Paul leaned back into the big chair that was clearly his. 'You don't believe in soul mates, then?' he said thoughtfully, still watching her.

She shook her head. 'No. It sounds wonderful, doesn't it, someone magically, spiritually linked to you down through the centuries, the one person you can be deliriously happy with, who fulfils every need? But no one can do that; it puts far too heavy a responsibility on the other person in the relationship. I think that anybody can probably fall in love with a whole lot of people—it's just luck as to which one they meet first.'

'So what is love at first sight, then?'

A dangerous delusion, she thought tartly. Aloud she said, 'Attraction. A physical thing.'

Physical definitely, but it had the power to ruin lives. Her mother had never really managed to forget the married man who had seduced her and then abandoned her when he'd got her pregnant.

Paul said, 'You believe that two people can look at each other and want each other—a *coup de foudre*, as my grandmother used to say?'

She restrained the instinct to move uneasily. 'I don't know what that means,' she equivocated.

Irony edged his voice. 'A thunderclap.'

'Oh.' Heat crept through her skin, because that was exactly how she'd felt when she'd seen him that first time in Fiji—as though a thunderclap had robbed her of her wits.

She said swiftly, 'Yes, that happens, but it's dangerous to think it's love.'

'But without it there can be no love. Not the sort of love that leads to marriage, anyway.'

He'd turned the screen off as soon as the drama had finished, so there was no sound but the soft, almost unheard sighing of the waves on the beach.

Hastily, because she wasn't accustomed to discussing desire and passion with men—especially not men like Paul—she said, 'I agree, but most psychologists seem to feel that there's a lot more to a happy marriage than s-sex.'

God, she was stuttering like an adolescent; the word seared itself into her brain.

'Or love,' Paul said blandly.

She shot him a quick, puzzled look.

He went on, 'People are more likely to form stable, happy relationships if they have the same values, even the same upbringing and social standing.'

'That sounds a bit cold-blooded,' she said. 'I think people can learn to love each other across class and cultural barriers.'

His brows lifted and a mocking smile tilted his mouth. 'Of course you do,' he said, the lightest flick of sarcasm underlining the words.

Greatly daring, Jacinta asked, 'Don't you?'

'I believe that nature does what's necessary to ensure the perpetuation of the species,' he said, his voice as indolent as his smile as he adroitly headed the conversation off into the discovery of a meteorite that suggested there could once have been life on Mars.

Later that night, Jacinta stood in her darkened bedroom and watched the stars wheel with monumental patience across the black sky, their steely light lending an air of mystery and glamour to the gardens.

How long had she known the owner of all this beauty? Not quite a week, because you couldn't count those few days in Fiji.

So according to her own firmly held beliefs she couldn't be falling in love. This complicated, overmastering blend of emotions that assailed her had to be nothing more than straight, unromantic physical attraction, whether you termed it sex, desire, or a hungry concupiscence.

Paul's cynical view of love was probably the correct one; her inner delight, that unfulfilled yearning, was merely the romantic glow Mother Nature flung over the driving need for humankind to reproduce.

If she wasn't careful she could become as obsessed with him as the doomed lovers in the television programme had been with each other.

And that would be stupid.

She should leave Waitapu.

Her heart clenched in her chest, but she knew she was right. It was too dangerous to stay.

Tomorrow she'd scan the ads in the newspaper and see if she could find a place to stay. Many of the flats let during term to university students would be empty now; perhaps she could rent one until the beginning of the new academic year.

She'd have to get a job and think of an excuse to leave.

Running away would complicate things, but if she stayed here she might end up very badly hurt.

She woke with a new and exciting plot twist burning in her brain, and without doing more than washing and dressing sat down in front of the computer, glad that she had an excuse not to go out to breakfast. However, she hadn't been typing for more than a few minutes when someone knocked sharply on her door.

'It's all right, Fran,' she called.

'It's not Fran, and it's not all right.'

She bit her lip, trying to control the sudden racing of her pulse. Reluctantly she got up from the desk.

Paul was dressed for work in a superbly tailored suit that reminded her he lived in an entirely different world from hers.

'What is it?' she said, not attempting to conceal the curtness in her query.

He looked at her with intent, measuring eyes. Then he smiled and her heart turned over. 'Come and have some breakfast,' he commanded pleasantly.

'I'm not really hungry,' she said, masking her uncertainty and exasperation with a crisp briskness. 'And I've just had a brilliant idea—I want to get it down before I forget it.'

His brows drew together. 'How long will it take?'

'Paul, I don't know.'

She'd said his name for the first time. It was like the finest wine on her tongue, complex and tangy and seductive, profoundly fascinating.

He laughed softly. 'All right, I'm sorry. But make sure you have something to eat when the inspiration's waned,' he said, and to her astonishment he picked up the hand clenched at her side and straightened out the tense fingers, running his thumb lightly across the terrified pulse in her narrow wrist.

White-faced, she jerked her hand free.

'I'll see you tonight,' he said evenly.

Jacinta didn't try to write until she heard the car go half an hour later. And only then, it seemed, was she able to breathe again.

'Oh, lord,' she said weakly.

Why had he done that? She cradled the hand he'd touched, looking at the fingers, her brain so utterly bemused she had to shake her head to force herself to move.

Paul's response startled her. If she'd refused to do anything Mark had suggested, he'd have tried to coax her, and if that hadn't worked he'd have insisted, and then sulked and made life uncomfortable for everyone. Paul had simply accepted her decision.

Of course, a cynical part of her brain reminded her, whether or not she ate breakfast with Paul made no real difference to his day. He might be a naturally dominant man, but he wasn't driven by Mark's lust to control.

She drifted into the kitchen and made herself a piece of

toast and a cup of coffee, then, ignoring Fran's dark look, wandered back to the bedroom and stood in the French window, eating the toast and drinking the coffee and gazing dreamily at the garden and the sea.

Eventually she forced herself free of the enchanted thraldom of Paul's touch and back into the world she'd created, but the magic stayed with her all day, at once appalling and transporting her, but also reinforcing her decision to leave Waitapu.

When she surfaced again around two, and arrived hungry and thirsty in the kitchen, Fran was coming in through the back door, carrying three large grocery bags.

'Haven't you had any lunch yet?' she asked, easing them down onto the bench. 'You'll get into bad habits if you don't train yourself better.'

'It's not exactly a matter of training,' Jacinta objected mildly, gathering ingredients together for a ham sandwich. 'Ideas come when they're ready.'

'I don't believe that. I think ideas come when you're ready. And erratic meals will ruin your digestion.'

Jacinta grinned. 'I know,' she said, 'and perhaps you're right. I'll try to train my ideas. Have you brought everything in? I'll go out—'

'No, no, that's all.' Fran opened the largest of the bags and hauled out a bag labelled 'couscous'.

'Here, I'll put that away.' Jacinta went to take it from her.

The housekeeper said serenely, 'Jacinta, make that sandwich. It's far quicker for me to stow everything away myself than it is to tell you where it goes.'

Jacinta sighed. 'Oh, all right,' she said. 'You keep all the exciting jobs for yourself.'

She sat down at the table, assembled a large sandwich, and began to demolish it while Fran stored an interesting selection of items in the pantry.

'Paul told me this morning,' Fran said, frowning at a bottle with green detergent in it, 'that he's having a party here this Saturday. As there'll be a couple of guests staying I had to do some preliminary buying.'

The ham and crisp greens from the herb garden turned tasteless as dry rice in Jacinta's mouth. Swallowing, she said, 'That's short notice.'

'Very,' Fran said dryly. 'Still, it's not his fault. Something went wrong with his arrangements, I imagine, because although he does most of his personal entertainment here, Paul's not one for bringing business home.'

'Will you be able to manage? I'm a reasonable plain cook—'

Fran gave her a swift smile. 'Oh, we always use a caterer.'

Naturally. Jacinta laughed and resumed eating, although more slowly. 'So this is the film party,' she said, trying to sound as though she wasn't fishing.

'Yes. Paul had something to do with organising the finances for the joint venture.' She sighed dramatically, rolling her eyes. 'Harry Moore's coming. Fancy having him here! Do you like his acting?'

'He's very good,' said Jacinta, who'd seen him in one film.

'Well, you'll be able to find out if the real man lives up to the man on the screen.'

Jacinta looked up. 'I won't be here,' she said, adding as Fran's eyebrows rose, 'unless I can help with the waiting. I used to be quite good at that.'

The housekeeper shrugged, then said comfortably, 'Oh, well, we'll see. But no, we won't need any extra waitresses.'

Which sent Jacinta into the conservatory to check out the vacancy ads in the day's paper. Most were of the 'Flatmate Wanted' variety, and there weren't many of those, either. After her experience with Mark, who'd persuaded her to join him in a mixed flat—only mixed, she discovered, after she'd arrived to join Mark and another man—

she wanted all-female flatmates. And doing it that way she wouldn't have to pay out a month's rent for a deposit.

After taking down the numbers of a couple of the most likely looking, she went out onto the terrace and sat for a long time watching the slow, smooth glide of the fish in the pond.

She should go and ring those numbers.

She wasn't going to.

For once in her life, she thought, dipping her hand into the cool water so that the fish could nibble her fingers, she wasn't going to listen to common sense.

The pond was big enough to take one splendid waterlily, a tropical hybrid that held huge, spiky violet flowers above the still surface. There was nothing sensible about that flower, she thought now, looking at it. It bloomed with defiant, sensuous immediacy.

For years she had put her life on hold. She'd willingly made that sacrifice for her mother, and she didn't regret it at all, but coming to Waitapu had shown her that she'd spent that time deliberately damping down her emotions because it hurt too much to give them free rein. She'd channelled all her energy, all her vitality, into helping her mother.

And because there was nothing she could do about it, she'd ignored that sense of life running past her with little to show for it but inevitable death.

Even finishing her degree had been fulfilling her mother's plan.

Now she wanted to live, to feel with all that was in her, to experience the sharp tang of life, to fall in love...

As she watched the goldfish cruise calmly, serenely, bloodlessly back and forth she accepted that she would be hurt. But before that she would learn to live again.

Oh, she wouldn't embarrass Paul with her emotions; she had too much pride to make herself ridiculous. But she'd enjoy them for what they were, and when the time came to go she'd do it with dignity.

She was lying on the lounger outside her room when the sound of an engine warned her that Paul was home. Delight and a desperate eagerness warred with discretion; in the end she stayed on the lounger, pretending to read the sheets she'd printed that day.

The small sounds of the homestead became suddenly heavy with significance. Listening to the tui singing from its perch on the grevillea and a door that slammed somewhere in the house, Jacinta had to consciously discipline her breathing. Nothing, however, could calm the racing chatter of her heartbeat, or dampen the slow curl of excitement at the base of her spine.

Yet strained though her ears were, she didn't hear him walk along the verandah, so that when he said, 'Good afternoon,' her fingers loosened and a couple of sheets of paper dropped onto the floor.

'I'm sorry,' he said, and stooped to pick them up, handing them to her without looking at them, for which she was extremely grateful.

'I didn't hear you,' she said inanely.

'So I see. Perhaps I should whistle. Although you might mistake me for Dean then.'

Grabbing for her composure, she managed to produce a laugh. 'Yes, I might. I suppose it's all the whistling he does at his dogs.'

'Possibly,' he said, blue eyes limpidly unreadable. 'Do you mind if I join you?'

'No, not at all.' And because she felt defenceless sprawled along the lounger, her faded cotton shorts revealing far too much skin, she swung her legs down and straightened up as he sat in a big rattan chair.

'Have you had a good day?' he asked.

'Fine. And you?'

Just ordinary pleasantries, the small coinage of conversation, yet nothing sounded ordinary or small when Paul spoke.

'Busy,' he said. 'Did Fran tell you about the party this weekend?'

'Yes. I offered to help her, but she didn't think you'd need a waitress or a good plain cook.'

Something glittered beneath his lashes, disappearing so swiftly she couldn't discern it. 'No,' he said blandly. 'The caterer will organise that side of things. I expect you to be a guest.'

No doubt it was kindly meant, although she wondered at the inflexible note in the words. 'Paul,' she said, feeling her way, 'it's very generous and hospitable of you to include me, but I really don't think I'd fit in.'

'If it's clothes—'

'It's not just that,' she said quietly.

'So tell me what it is.'

It was a command, not a suggestion. She said, 'I'd feel that I'd imposed on your hospitality. Would you have asked me if I'd been staying at the bach?'

His smile was hard and sardonic. 'Yes.'

She cast around for another objection. 'Is Dean coming?'

Two lines grooved vertically between his brows, strengthening his subtle air of intimidation. 'Dean will be away this weekend with Brenda. Have you met her yet?'

'No. She's busy with exams, apparently.' It was a side-track; she went on, 'I'd rather not, Paul.'

'I'd like you to.'

If he'd been at all arrogant about his request—if he'd said it as though she owed him for his hospitality—she'd have refused him. After all, she could ask Dean for the loan of his cottage while he was away.

But she couldn't resist. Or the smile that accompanied it, oddly sympathetic.

So, perhaps helped by remembering the sari she and her mother had chosen in Fiji—that glittering, beautiful thing of glorious orange-gold that somehow transformed her skin into ivory and her hair into amber, and set the dancing lights gleaming in her eyes—she said, 'All right.'

His smile was ironic, as though he was laughing at both her and himself. 'You'll have fun,' he promised.

Jacinta hadn't been to a party for years. She'd never been to a party with Hollywood film stars; it would be something to tell her children, if she ever had any. 'I'm sure I will,' she agreed.

CHAPTER SIX

PAUL left for Auckland the next morning and didn't return for the rest of the week.

A good thing, Jacinta told herself stubbornly, settling into a calm rhythm of writing and swimming and walking, talking to Dean and Fran—even helping the housekeeper in the garden, although a gardener worked there three days a week.

She might be poised on the brink of falling in love, but she didn't need to go looking for trouble—and that was what she'd do if Paul was there all the time. His absence gave her a breathing space, time to compose herself.

Time to miss him.

The manuscript dawdled along—partly because she often found herself dreaming as she stared at the computer screen, dreams that had nothing to do with the characters she was striving to bring to life. But also because she'd reached an impasse; although she knew what the novel's protagonists had to do, she found to her irritation and indignation that they weren't satisfied with the plot she and her mother had mapped out for them. They sulked and fumed and had to be forced along their preordained paths, and in the process they turned wooden and obstructive and banal.

Jacinta set her chin and struggled on.

Three days before the party she took out the sari from the wardrobe. The short-sleeved blouse in orange silk fitted her well, settling snugly at her waist. She remembered how to get into the soft folds of the skirt, and then draped herself in the silk veil in citrus colours of mandarin and gold and bright, clear orange.

It wasn't her usual style. The Hindu woman in the hot little shop had been an excellent saleswoman, aided as she'd been by Cynthia Lyttelton's cries of delight and pleasure when Jacinta had modelled the sari. Jacinta had only allowed herself to be persuaded because the vivid colours did such amazing things to her skin and eyes and hair.

As she turned away to take it off she remembered with a brittle smile that she'd bought it the day after Paul had danced with her.

Her sandals, of tan leather, had the right oriental air, although to really set the costume off she needed jewellery. She'd have to do without, because apart from a pair of gold hoop earrings she had none. Even her mother's wedding ring had been buried with her, a pathetic reminder of the lengths she'd gone to in order to keep the censorious at bay in the small town where Jacinta had grown up.

Replacing the sari in the wardrobe, she hoped fervently that the guests at Paul's party didn't turn up in shorts and bathing suits!

On Friday the caterers arrived and took over the kitchen. Although Fran complained about the mess, she revelled in the confusion, even bringing Jacinta's lunch to her on a tray so that she wouldn't get in their way.

The caterers drove back to Auckland that night, and Jacinta waited for Paul's car, but at seven the phone rang. Jacinta knew who it was even before she picked up the receiver.

'Has Fran got you on answering duty?' Paul asked.

'No, I was going past when I realised the answering machine hadn't been switched on.'

He said, 'I see. I'm in Sydney at the moment, but I'll be home tomorrow morning.'

'I'll tell Fran,' she said, listening to the slow thud of her heart.

'All well?'

'Yes, everything's fine.'

'Are the caterers under control?'

Jacinta laughed. 'Under Fran's control, certainly. She's enjoying herself very much.'

'She likes bossing people around,' he said dryly. 'And are you enjoying yourself very much?'

'Yes, of course.'

A voice from his background called out: a female voice.

'I have to go now,' he said. 'See you tomorrow.'

Jacinta replaced the receiver, telling herself that the gripping pang in her heart was not jealousy. It couldn't be because she had no reason to be jealous. The woman in the background could easily be a secretary. Sydney was in Australia's eastern time zone, two hours behind New Zealand, so it would be just after five there.

Or she could be a friend's wife. Or a relative—once he'd mentioned cousins in Australia.

Except that the tone of her voice had been seductive rather than businesslike or friendly.

That night the long, wakeful hours dragged by, illuminated by the vivid imaginings of Jacinta's brain as she spun scenarios of Paul with a beautiful woman...

She should have stuck to her original plan and left Waitapu.

When she couldn't bear it any longer she got up and tried to write, but nothing would come, and she wondered whether she was just fooling herself and wasting time with the manuscript.

She began to read it, and it was boring—hackneyed characters in hackneyed situations, clumsily constructed sentences and dull conversation, action sequences that read with all the power and fire of treacle. In disgust she put the sheets back on the desk and went to bed again, and this time she slept.

Only for a short time, however. She woke early, swam until she was exhausted and then, unable even to look at the computer, wandered around the garden to the hammock suspended from the wide branches of a jacaranda tree. It was hung for Paul's long legs, and at the thought of him sleeping in it something clutched her stomach.

After several attempts she managed to climb into it and lay sprawled in its shady embrace, staring up into the feathery dome of the tree.

The sound of her name woke her.

'Oh,' she said feebly, opening her eyes to meet Paul's cobalt gaze.

He'd been frowning, but it faded, so all she saw were the two kinks in his brows as they straightened. Her spine melted.

'You hid yourself well,' he said evenly. He was standing beside the trunk of the tree, and as she lifted herself on her elbow he leaned back against the bark, the small movement emphasising the slight shifting and coiling of his heavily-muscled thighs beneath fine cotton trousers.

Jacinta swallowed. 'What time is it?'

'Just on midday.'

'Good lord!' She sat up, clutching the side of the hammock as it swayed. He reached out a hand and steadied it, regarding her with an enigmatic half-smile. 'I didn't sleep terribly well last night,' she explained.

'Why not?'

'No reason.' She swung her legs over the side and got out, not without some difficulty because the wretched hammock would have thrown her if Paul hadn't held it still. 'Did you have a good trip?' she asked, slightly red-faced when at last she was standing up.

'Excellent, thank you. Come and have some lunch with me. We've been banished to the verandah.'

Just before they reached the table Paul said, 'I saw something in Sydney that might be useful for you,' and detoured into his room.

Keeping her eyes averted, Jacinta waited until he

emerged through the French windows with a parcel. It was a book on the techniques of writing novels.

'Oh,' she said, scanning the index eagerly, 'thank you so much! I've read a couple of how-to books from the university library, but this one looks great. I need it too. I'm stuck.'

'I believe it happens all the time,' Paul said, smiling as she flicked through the pages.

Embarrassed, she put the book down on the table and said, 'Thank you, Paul. I'll read it with great interest.'

'I hope it gets you through your block,' he said easily. 'Sit down. We'd better eat before Fran comes to sweep everything away.'

'She's really in her element. I poked my nose in and offered to help, but they all shooed me out and told me to get lost—in the nicest possible manner, of course.'

He laughed. 'They're used to working together,' he said.

Lunch was a salad and quiche, with crusty brown bread and olives and sun-dried tomatoes. Paul drank a beer with it; Jacinta had mineral water, and tea afterwards.

They talked of nothing much. Although Paul was a little remote, happiness hummed through Jacinta, reverberating in every cell, oversetting the common-sense strictures of her mind in a flood of delight. The sea sparkled and scintillated beneath a sky of blazing blue, the small sparrows that waited on the verandah railings for crumbs glowed chestnut and buff in the golden light, and the panicles of lilac-tinted flowers in the cabbage tree—the biggest lily in the world—scented the air with a tropical fervour.

Jacinta asked, 'What time does this party start?'

'We're having a barbecue on the beach at eight. Two people are coming up around five. Laurence Perry is one of the character actors, and Meriam Anderson is the producer's assistant. They'll be staying overnight.'

She nodded. 'If it's a barbecue I suppose they'll be wearing shorts.' It wasn't hard to keep the disappointment from her voice, but he gave her a swift, keen glance.

'I wouldn't like to guess what they'll be wearing,' he said. 'Meriam Anderson dresses in a very understated manner, but I doubt if she'll be in shorts. She's English, and for her shorts are too informal to wear to any party, even a barbecue.'

He knows her very well, Jacinta thought, horrified by the shard of jealousy that pierced her body, so acute that it hurt even when she breathed.

He went on, 'However, Harry Moore's girlfriend, Liane, thinks that dressing formally means putting on another toe ring. I imagine you could wear a nightgown and they'd think nothing of it—beyond the fact that you were making a statement. They understand statements.'

Was her sari a statement? She had no idea, but she certainly wasn't going to wear any of her shorts, all of which showed their age badly.

'I'm wearing casual trousers and a shirt,' he said. 'No tie. Don't worry about them. They're just people.'

She finished the last of her tea and set the cup and saucer down. 'I know, I know, but I don't want to look like an oddity.'

'You won't.' He paused, then said, 'How you treat them will determine how they treat you. Beneath the hype and the beautiful faces and the money they're ordinary people.'

'Surely hype and money and beauty—not to mention power and talent—cut people out from the common herd? Harry Moore, for example, can't even go to a restaurant without being mobbed by fans. A few years of that—and the enormous amount of money he earns—is going to change him, even if he was just a simple farm boy to start with.'

Paul leaned back in his chair and surveyed her with half closed eyes, impenetrable beneath his surface amusement. 'He's intelligent and astute and he knows where he's going, but yes, I was being a bit flippant. Think of them, then, as another species—interesting and worth studying but ultimately not important.'

Because you're never going to meet them again, she thought, hurt—and yet of course he was right.

He added thoughtfully, 'Actually, with hair that colour you've probably had more than your fair share of attention. Do you think it's changed your character?'

'No,' she said. 'I'm a very ordinary person.'

His answering smile lightened her heart.

That night Jacinta dressed with great care. The material of the sari lent its light to her hair, changing unashamed ginger into a molten river of fire. She left her curls to riot and donned the gold earrings, then used a lipgloss she'd had for some years, a peachy-gold colour that made her lips seem fuller and more—interesting, she hoped.

In the grip of a helpless hope, she went out.

The two film people were still in their rooms, so she walked down the hall and into the morning room and across into the conservatory. She was looking down onto the beach, where a sheep was roasting on the spit in the charge of one of the caterer's staff, when some imperceptible alteration in the atmosphere brought her head around.

Paul stood in the open doors between the conservatory and the morning room. He was looking at her, dark brows drawn together, his face set into a rigid cast.

Tension leapt between them, stark, fierce.

I look awful, Jacinta thought, her barely born confidence ebbing into desolation.

And then, as though he'd cut it off, the moment was gone. 'Those colours suit you magnificently,' he said, the words spoken in a tone he might have used to praise a dog.

Rebuffed, she replied stiffly, 'Thank you.' Her smile was set and artificial as she fought to control the pain that slashed through her.

A light, feminine voice, English-accented, said, 'Paul, this is a wonderful place!'

He turned and smiled at the woman who'd followed him

into the room. Jacinta watched Meriam Anderson's response, as involuntary as hers, to the warmth of his smile. In her mid-thirties, and dressed, Jacinta noted, in a soft, navy blue silk dress that managed to look both casual and chic, the woman came across and slid her arm into Paul's, and nodded at Jacinta.

When they'd been introduced earlier that evening Jacinta had been in a blouse and the rusty skirt, and Meriam had been very gracious. But now, although her voice stayed warm and pleasant, her eyes narrowed slightly.

'My dear,' she said, 'what a splendid outfit. You look as though you're going to burst into flames any minute.'

The evening went downhill from there.

At least, Jacinta thought as people began to arrive and be conducted down to the beach, she no longer cared what they thought about her. There was only one man whose opinion meant anything to her, and he'd taken one look at her and switched off. No doubt he thought she was blatant and garish.

However, she was not going to let his rejection—if that was what it was—affect her.

Tilting her chin, she tried to ignore the gnawing ache in her heart. Eventually about sixty guests stood in the last rays of the sun, dressed with the sort of bravura chicness that made them stand out. Her outfit didn't look out of place at all. Not when Liane, Harry Moore's girlfriend, wore a black slip with nothing on underneath, and a fanfare of peacock's feathers in her black hair. Only one toe ring, Jacinta noticed, but that appeared to have a diamond in it.

It was definitely a collection of beautiful people. Amazingly good-looking in a sombre, brooding way, Harry Moore was Jacinta's height, with a mouth that was saved from sulkiness by a humorous quirk. He flirted with Jacinta, but then he flirted with all the other women there except Liane. Her he looked at with a desperate yearning he tried to hide.

I know what it's like, Jacinta thought, and applied herself to the conversation, hoping to help him through whatever private hell he was enduring.

'With that colouring you have to be Irish,' he declared, and when she'd cheerfully disclaimed any Celtic blood, he said, 'I'll bet there's some in your background. You look like a high summer heatwave, sultry and exuberant and lush.'

His moody dark eyes surveyed her with a sensual appreciation that made his career as a screen heart-throb inevitable.

Jacinta smiled as she thanked him, thinking ironically that if you were worried about social graces, wearing a broken heart made evenings like this ridiculously easy because it was impossible to care what people thought of you.

Except for one person, and his opinion had been only too plain. Her eyes searched the crowd, now noisily talking and laughing, and found Paul. He was standing a little apart, talking to two men who, although they wore similar cotton trousers and short-sleeved shirts to every other man there, had 'suits' written all over them.

Against Paul's effortless authority Harry looked somehow unformed, a man in the making. And yet he was her age, almost thirty, not all that much younger than Paul, who had probably been born with that uncompromising aura of dominance. It was something to do with inner strength, a confidence so firmly rooted in character that it was unbreakable.

And a sexual promise that drew her and every other woman there with its subtle, powerful lure. What had happened to turn him off like that? He'd taken one look at her and despised her; she'd seen the swift flash of cold contempt in his eyes before the shutters came down and blocked her out.

She spent the next hour listening to Harry Moore. He drank more than she liked, and although his eyes followed his girlfriend as she flitted from group to group he stayed close to Jacinta, making her laugh with tales of happenings—most funny, but some appalling—on the sets of various films he'd made.

Eventually his girlfriend came back, and Jacinta took the opportunity to move across to Laurence Perry, the pleasantly ugly middle-aged actor who was also staying the night. He gave her a ravaged, intense smile and observed, 'I envy you living in this magnificent place.'

Jacinta's answering smile would probably be engraved on her face for days. 'I'm just visiting, unfortunately. Have you enjoyed your stay in New Zealand?'

His glance moved to the slim woman at Paul's side. 'Very much,' he said. 'You know, when we met this afternoon I thought you reminded me of someone and I couldn't work out who it was until I saw you wrapped in that gauzy golden robe.'

Jacinta fixed an interested look to her face. 'Do I have a double?'

'Not exactly a double, but a hundred or so years ago there was someone who looked very like you,' Laurence said, shrewd eyes studying her. 'My grandmother had a print of a picture painted by a Victorian, one of the Pre-Raphaelites. It's called *Flaming June* and shows a bare-armed girl sleeping; she had your high-bridged nose and soft mouth, and she was your colouring too. As well, she was draped in a cloth the exact orange-gold in your veil.'

Jacinta lifted her brows. 'How intriguing,' she said, her voice steady. Paul and Meriam were making their way towards them, and she'd noted the way the other woman's hand was clinging to his arm. Anguish twisted inside her; she said, 'I must see if I can track down a copy. I wonder if she was teased as much as I was because of her ginger hair.'

'Did they call you Carrots?'

She surprised herself by producing a wry little laugh.

'Oh, yes. All sorts of variations on the theme of carrots and gingerbread.'

'But now you have the last word,' he said, and smiled at her surprise. 'Most of them would probably give their eye-teeth to have green eyes and luminous ivory skin and hair like yours,' he said, embarrassing her.

'I doubt it,' she said. 'Buying sunscreen to stop me burning makes me prohibitively expensive to keep.' And she flushed as she realised how provocative her comment might sound.

Just as Paul and Meriam came up he grinned and said, 'But worth it, surely?'

'Worth what?' Meriam said, looking alertly from one to the other.

'Worth spending an inordinate amount of money on sunblock to protect that glorious skin,' Laurence said promptly.

Jacinta hadn't looked at Paul; his tone came as an unpleasant surprise. 'Indeed it is,' he drawled, each word like a tiny whip scoring deep into her composure.

Although Meriam Anderson wasn't beautiful, she wore her hair and make-up and clothes with a panache that made up for her lack of looks. 'Thank heavens we live in a time when we have sunblocks,' she said then. 'Paul, you throw a wonderful party. What would you say if I asked to stay an extra couple of days?'

'I'd be delighted. Is there any chance of that?'

'Sadly, no,' she sighed. 'But I'll take a raincheck on the invitation, Paul.'

He smiled at her. Jacinta drew in an uneven breath.

Without trying, she thought, suddenly defenceless against him, he dominated the whole scene. All right, he was clever and handsome, but these people were sophisticated and worldly, and used to the authority and power that money gave, and yet none of them could hold a candle to him.

Even Harry Moore's girlfriend was watching him with an intent, speculative look.

Well, Jacinta was not going to let her own heated yearning and acute awareness of Paul spoil this occasion. It was probably the only time in her life she'd be at a gathering like this, and she was determined to at least appreciate it.

Paul stayed with Meriam. Neither was overt or obvious, unlike Liane, who was now wound around Harry; however, it was perfectly clear that they found each other very interesting.

I am not in love with him, Jacinta told herself as she circulated. *I am not.* Not now, not ever.

But as the evening wore on she found it more and more difficult to keep up the pretence. If it hadn't seemed like an obscure form of surrender she'd have sneaked quietly away after they'd eaten dinner—superb and succulent meat from the spit, fish wrapped in taro leaves and baked in coals, salads that were miracles of taste and freshness, and fruit, cleverly laid out on a table covered with the fronds of New Zealand's native palm and the vivid, incandescent flowers of hibiscuses.

She stuck it out, although later, when she came to sort out her recollections, she found she remembered very little. However, she spoke to everyone there, surprised at how polite and pleasant and interested in her they all seemed.

You didn't know it but you're a snob, she thought when at last she decided that she'd had enough, late enough in the evening for pride to be properly salvaged. You thought they'd all be crass and snobbish and aggressive, like the worst and most newsworthy of Hollywood stars.

Paul and Meriam were talking to a couple of the money men. She'd have liked to leave without anyone noticing, but even as the thought whisked through her mind Paul looked up, his eyes resting on her face with unsettling dispassion. He said something to the others and left them, walking towards her with lithe grace.

An hour or so previously a little wind had sprung up

from the sea, and everyone had moved onto the lawn, where the trees sheltered them. In spite of the sea breeze it was still very warm, and the guests had reached that pleasant stage where they were enjoying themselves without tension.

Except for her. And the cause of her tension was walking towards her, his hair gleaming silver in the lights.

'I've had a wonderful party, but if you don't mind I'll slip away now,' she said when he got closer.

'Before anyone else?'

The implied criticism made her stiffen. 'No one's going to miss me,' she said.

'Oh, I think they might. You've been a definite hit. Liane has decided you're a threat to her power over Harry.'

She drew in a swift breath, trying to ignore the soft, cynical drawl. 'She's very insecure,' she said. 'It's been great—fascinating—'

'But you've had enough.'

Jacinta looked up, caught the glitter of his eyes, the hard line of his mouth, a line that gentled into a smile, coaxing, half-rueful, completely compelling. 'No, of course not,' she said, surrendering.

He looked past her. 'Good,' he said, adding, 'It won't be long now anyway. Here comes the coffee.'

He was right. Everyone drank coffee, and soon, amid a flurry of trans-Pacific farewells and best wishes, the convoy of cars left the homestead for Auckland.

'A great evening,' Laurence Perry declared as the last one left. 'Thank you, Paul, for more excellent Kiwi hospitality. I'm turning in.'

'I don't feel like going to bed yet,' Meriam said with a half-laugh. 'I'm wired. It's such a beautiful night, I'd like to go for a walk.'

'Why not?' Paul's deep, beautiful voice was lazily amused.

Jacinta turned away. 'Goodnight,' she said. 'I'll see you in the morning.'

Thank heavens she could retire to her bedroom and close the doors and pull the curtains so that no one could see her.

And thank heavens that even the most shattering emotions eventually gave way to sleep.

A sleep that was disturbed much later by a woman's laughter, and the sound of light footsteps on the verandah. Meriam, she thought; Paul moved noiselessly. But then she heard Paul's voice, and immediately stuffed her head under her pillow.

When she finally emerged from the sanctuary of her pillow all was silent again except for the soft whispering of a wind playing along the wooden fretwork lace above the verandah. For some reason she got up to pull the curtains more tightly, and saw a light glimmering across the floor of the verandah. It came from Paul's room.

It needn't mean anything, she thought desperately, closing her eyes against it. Perhaps he couldn't sleep either. He didn't strike her as promiscuous—but then he could have been conducting an affair with Meriam for months, all the time the film company had been in New Zealand.

Neither he nor the producer's assistant were the sort of person who proclaimed their emotions, but they'd definitely been 'together' the preceding night. Whether that togetherness had extended to the bedroom she had no way of knowing.

And where did that leave the actress Gerard had pointed out to her in Ponsonby?

It's none of your business, she told herself drearily, turning away to crawl back into bed.

She woke late, so late that the house was silent around her, and when she came out the guests were gone, and Paul with them. The caterers had cleaned up and gone the night before, so that all that was left of the party was the darker green of the lawn where it had been crushed by feet.

For the first time Jacinta wondered just how much

money Paul had. Such quiet, efficient service was expensive, but more than that, it was difficult to find. Even a housekeeper was hard to get.

Paul could buy such service, apparently without worrying about the cost.

Of course, she thought desolately, he'd been born to this. She had grown up with poverty. And yet in many ways they had a lot in common. New Zealand didn't have much of a class system—

'Oh, for heaven's *sake*!' she said aloud, furious with herself for spinning dreams out of gossamer.

They had nothing in common, and he couldn't have made that plainer the night before.

After she'd eaten toast and fruit for breakfast, she went for a long walk and then settled down in the lounger outside her room to read some of the book he'd bought her. Of course she knew what she was doing; she was waiting.

But after a while the book began to make sense to her. She read and reread a couple of pages and put it down, staring sightlessly out into the sunlight. Ideas began to collect in her mind, too bright to resist. She got to her feet and set off for the computer.

Hours later she came back to herself, thinking exultantly, Yes!

It was good; she knew it was good.

She saved everything, backed it up and stretched, yawning. Suddenly ravenous, she looked at her watch. It was half past two, so for once Fran had forgotten about her.

In the kitchen Jacinta made herself a sandwich—cheese and tomato and cress, with a touch of Fran's pesto. Taking it out across the lawn, she sat down in the gazebo and applied herself to eating it, forcing the food over the lump in her chest.

When she'd finished she drank a glass of the orange juice that Fran squeezed every morning, concentrating ferociously on the thick, delicious freshness, the combination of sweet and tangy flavours, the way it eased across her tongue and down her throat, because that was the only way she could deal with this—this despair that had been lying in wait for her ever since she'd woken.

She wanted to wail and shriek and beat her breast and stamp her feet at the total unfairness of the world, at her own stupidity in falling in love with a man who was not for her.

But, even as she imagined herself losing control so appallingly, a reluctant, unwilling smile tugged at her mouth.

'I seem to remember reading something about how pleasant it is to come upon a woman smiling to herself.' Paul's voice was studied and speculative as he walked around the corner of the gazebo, past the scented, smothering flowers of the rose that draped itself artistically across the white-painted timber.

Jacinta's heart leapt. 'It sounds Victorian,' she said, hoping her voice was as steady as his.

'Sentimental?' The sun gleamed on his hair, caught the vivid depths of his eyes and picked out the arrogant, hard-planed contours of his face.

She smiled again. It was difficult, but she thought she carried it off rather well. 'The Victorians often were sentimental.'

'Agreed.' He scrutinised her with an oddly measuring look, as though he was superimposing another's features on hers, and said, 'Yes, I see what Laurence meant last night. You have the kind of face the Pre-Raphaelites loved to paint.'

It didn't exactly sound like a compliment, and yet his glance lingered a second too long on her mouth. Jacinta's pulse picked up speed.

'I'm flattered,' she returned politely. There followed an unnerving moment of silence, one she broke by asking, 'Have you just come back?'

'About five minutes ago. I took them down to the airport and sent them on their way. What have you been doing?'

'Writing,' she said succinctly, and added, 'And I must

thank you again for the book you bought. I read a couple of chapters, and while I was going through a list of dos and don'ts I realised where I was going wrong.'

'Good,' he said, and leaned over to pick a rose from the edge of the gazebo. 'It's the same colour as your hair,' he said, tucking it in behind her ear. Her ear and scalp tingled, and she thought she could feel his touch right to the roots of her hair.

Hair couldn't feel, she reminded herself feverishly, it was dead—but the effects of that moment of closeness rippled down her spine in a shiver of delight.

Eyes half closed, he stepped back and surveyed her. 'Yes, exactly the same colour. So the manuscript is coming along well?'

'I think it is,' she said cautiously, and astonished herself by confiding, 'I've been trying to follow the plot my mother and I worked out, but it was really difficult; when I reread what I'd written it dragged horribly. The book said that if the characters wouldn't do what the writer wanted them to, the writer should give them a chance and see what happened.'

He nodded, blue eyes keen and perceptive. 'And what has happened?'

'Well,' she said ruefully, 'it's heading in a completely different direction from the one Mum and I mapped out.'

'And that worries you?'

She looked down at her hands. 'Yes,' she said quietly, 'I suppose that's why I've resisted it. I feel as though I've cut loose from my mother. Abandoned her, in fact. The book was to be a memorial to her, but if I do follow the characters it won't be the book she loved and helped create.'

'I see,' he said thoughtfully. 'But, you know, you'll never produce anything worthwhile if you don't take it for your own. We can't live other people's lives for them, or produce other people's work.'

Once more surprised at how perceptive he was, she nodded. Although he probably owed his career to his understanding of people's motives and actions.

'I didn't know I had this itch to write,' she said. An itch so powerful that even when her emotional life was in turmoil she was almost able to ignore it while she wrote.

And ease some of the pain by treating it as material for her work.

'How do you go about it?' he asked.

'At first I tried to write each sentence perfectly, but that was impossible, so now I'm getting everything down as quickly as I can, and then I'll go back and tidy it up and cut out the padding and put in the bits I need to expand on.'

'And then?'

She stared at him. 'What do you mean?'

His gaze was a cool blue challenge. 'Where do you plan to send it?'

'I hadn't—'

'Don't tell me you're going to spend three months writing it and then put it in the bottom of your wardrobe for the rest of your life!'

Uncertainly, she said, 'I don't know how good it is.'

'You're not likely to ever find out until you send it off,' he said with matter-of-fact directness. 'I assume that's what your mother wanted you to do?'

Jacinta hesitated. 'I suppose so. We never discussed it.'

'Most writing is done for publication.'

'Do you realise what you've done?' she demanded, half-angry and half-exhilarated at this new idea. 'I'd never really thought of anyone else reading it. Now every time I sit down to write I'll see the public sitting on my shoulder.'

'Inhibiting you?'

'Well—no,' she said. 'At least, I hope not.'

He looked at her for several seconds, his mouth straight and almost grim, before saying calmly, 'I'd certainly give it a go. You're enjoying doing it, aren't you?'

'Mostly,' she admitted. 'When I'm not so frustrated I could jump up and down with rage.'

'I believe that's the way it happens,' he said. 'Let's go for a walk. You probably need it and I certainly do. I'm leaving for Europe tomorrow, and I have a very busy week ahead.'

Loneliness clawed her. Trying to sound normal, she said, 'I'd love to see Europe. Especially France and Italy.'

'You'll get there one day.' He held out his hand and automatically she accepted it; it was strong and warm, not the hand of a man who spent all day indoors. He swam, she knew, but from the calluses on his hands he also did some heavy work.

She stepped away and he relinquished his grip, but not before she caught a glimpse of some fugitive emotion beneath the dark lashes, a coldly calculating gleam that chilled her.

'Tell me,' he said as they started along the beach, 'how you got to know Gerard well enough to accept his offer of help.'

Choosing her words carefully, she said, 'He'd been my tutor since the beginning of the year, so we knew each other. He found me sound asleep in the library one night.'

'Sleeping in the library isn't uncommon,' Paul said, 'especially just before exams.'

'No.'

'So Gerard invited you to live with him.' His voice was amused, almost bland, yet an uneasy little shiver tightened her skin.

'Hardly,' she said dryly. 'He bought me a cup of coffee.'

'And then he asked you to live with him?'

A seagull ran to within a few feet of them, surveying them with greedy, bright eyes. Keeping her eyes on it, Jacinta said, 'Of course he didn't. He offered to drive me home.'

Another silence, heavy with unspoken thoughts, a silence that compelled her to add, 'I refused, so he insisted on getting me a taxi.'

That was when she'd choked back tears, too exhausted to exert her usual control over her emotions and well aware that Mark was probably waiting for her, ready for another scene like that of the previous evening, when he'd raged at her almost all night. She'd found a temporary place to stay with a friend, but she wasn't able to move until the following week; she had been dreading the intervening days.

'I believe you were having trouble with a relationship,' Paul observed.

'I—how do you know?'

'Gerard,' he said laconically.

'I didn't tell him anything about—about that.'

He paused, then said judicially, 'Presumably he guessed.'

Jacinta bit her lip. 'Yes.'

'And Gerard suggested you move into his spare bedroom.'

Irritation spurred her into a snappy answer. 'Only because his cleaning service had let him down in a big way again. He told me that if I kept house and cooked his meals I could have the spare bedroom for free, but I...' The words trailed away.

One of Paul's greatest assets in his career had to be that warm, almost sympathetic voice; it was too easy to be lulled into confiding things you regretted later.

He said, 'So then he found a flat for you.'

'That was a piece of luck! And as it's not too far from the apartment he was living in I could take up his offer of a job.'

He sent her a heavy-lidded glance. 'Very fortunate,' he said non-committally. 'Gerard seems to be satisfied with the bargain.'

'I hope so. He's been very kind.'

'Not by his reckoning,' he said, his aloof tone unsettling

her. 'Tell me, is this arrangement going to continue at his new house?'

'Yes, but there's a small flat at the back. I'm going to be like Fran and live on the job.' And if there was a hint of defiance in her tone she hoped he noticed it. She objected to being cross-examined as though she was a hostile witness.

'And will you enjoy that?'

'It'll be wonderful to have a place to call my own, even if it isn't.'

'Of course, you're helping Gerard too,' he said thoughtfully.

'Well, of course.' Gerard had been a rock at a very stressful time, and she'd always be grateful to him.

CHAPTER SEVEN

PAUL said abruptly, 'It sounds the ideal arrangement.' And waited a second too long before adding, 'Except for one where you wouldn't need to worry about money at all.'

Jacinta stopped herself from shrugging. 'That would be perfect, but it's difficult to arrange nowadays.'

He didn't frown but she felt as though he did. Ridiculous, she thought despairingly.

When he spoke his voice was cool. 'If you don't know what you're going to do with this degree, why did you do it?'

'It seemed the logical thing to do when I left school. I loved history—it was my best subject—and I didn't have the foggiest idea of any sort of career. My mother wanted me to go to university.' She flushed but went on steadily, 'She'd started a degree but wasn't able to finish it, and she blamed herself because she couldn't manage without me after my first two years. It was her ambition to have me capped and gowned, even if it had to be after her death. And—in a way going back to university was convenient; I'd spent years at home and I was—afraid, I suppose—of trying to find a job.'

And that was something she hadn't admitted, even to herself, before.

'Forgive me if this is intrusive, but do you not have a father to call on?'

She said steadily, 'He was killed in a boating accident before I was born, but I have no idea who he was. My mother would never tell me.' It was probably his silence, and the understanding she thought she sensed in him, that emboldened her to continue, 'She just said that he wasn't free.' She'd also said she'd fallen wholly and embarrassingly in love. 'I've always assumed he was married.'

'It certainly sounds like it,' he murmured. 'It must have been tough growing up without a father.'

'It was tougher on her. She brought me up, and worked damned hard to do it.' Startled by the unexpected note of fierceness in her voice, she added lamely, 'She had a difficult life, and it doesn't seem fair that she should die so wretchedly. And don't tell me that life isn't fair.'

'I don't deal in platitudes,' he said, 'especially with someone like you, who's had to face that particular injustice for too many years.'

'I'd like to have been able to repay her for some of her sacrifices. Almost the only pleasure she got out of those last years was thinking of the things I'd be able to do when she died, and quite frankly it stinks!'

She knew she sounded childish, but she couldn't control the sudden, furious outburst. As angry tears started to her eyes she groped in her pocket for a handkerchief.

'It does,' he said gently, holding out a beautifully pressed white one.

Jacinta took it and blew her nose defiantly. 'The worst thing,' she muttered, unable to stop herself from divulging this, 'was that when she died I was relieved.'

'It's all right,' he said, and to her astonishment pulled her into his arms, effortlessly subduing her first resistance until in the end she gave in and leaned against him, desperate to absorb a measure of his calm, quiet strength.

Sheltered in the powerful cage of his embrace, she relaxed, her head coming to rest naturally on his shoulder. His faint, potent scent and the warmth of his skin, the solid bulwark of his body, combined to work an elemental magic. Although Jacinta knew this unspoken compassion was just as dangerous as the wildfire need that consumed her night and day, she couldn't wrest herself away from the hazardous lure of his unfaltering steadiness. Boneless, without volition, she was unable to follow the commands of that tiny part of her brain that could still think.

Eventually common sense returned, and she muttered, 'I'm sorry,' as she steeled herself to pull away.

A lean hand stroked the strands of hair back from her hot cheek and neck. 'Have you really cried for her?' he asked, his voice deep and soothing.

'I— I—'

He couldn't have asked anything more likely to break down the floodgates. How long he supported her while she wept into his cotton shirt she didn't know, but she'd never felt so safe.

Eventually it finished, and this time he let her go.

'I'm sorry,' she mumbled again, refusing to look at him as she tried to tidy away the signs of her grief.

'Why?' He took her arm and turned her around. 'What you need,' he said with cool assurance, 'is a cup of tea. And probably something for a headache.'

'You've done this before,' she said, trying to smile.

'Occasionally. But every Kiwi—even our coffee generation—turns to tea in an emergency.'

He made it for her, drank a cup with her, and followed her lead when she asked him his opinion of the newly announced team for the Commonwealth Games.

That was when she realised that her initial fierce, hopeless attraction, that first violent fervour, was now buttressed by the love growing deep inside her, a love that joined with her sexual awakening, reinforcing it.

Because Paul had to catch an early flight the next morning he left as the stars began to prick holes in the sky; he'd spend the night in his flat. Jacinta wished him luck and waved goodbye, and then trailed into the huge, empty house.

The next week was oddly busy, yet serene and peaceful. The aftermath of her bout of tears was a calm acceptance she'd been lacking before. Her mother was dead; she'd done whatever it was she'd been put on earth to do, and now had left it all behind her.

That recognition renewed a forgotten energy. Jacinta began to plan a future, a future that didn't include Paul. Although she missed him with every cell in her body, longing for him through the endless night hours until shadows darkened the fine skin beneath her eyes, the stark pragmatism she'd inherited from her mother told her that in spite of his kindness he wasn't in love with her.

He'd almost certainly made love to Meriam Anderson the night of the party; if he'd felt anything at all for Jacinta he wouldn't have done that.

No, he was not for her.

That being so, she'd have to organise her life.

What she wanted to do, she admitted, was stay at Waitapu and write. A pretty pipe-dream, but she could write anywhere.

If she gave up university and used the rest of her mother's inheritance, she could rent a small flat in a small town somewhere and buy what furniture she needed as well as a second-hand computer and printer. She couldn't expect Gerard to continue lending her his, and, although the arrangement she had with him would be ideal, he might not want to continue it when she told him she was giving up her MA.

Of course he might, and that would be great.

But if he didn't she'd have to get a job so that she didn't starve, and jobs were notoriously difficult to get in small towns. Especially for people with no commercial qualifications.

Perhaps she should use the money to go to a polytech and qualify in some field that would pay her a living wage. That would be sensible.

Unfortunately, all possible careers filled her with dismay. In spite of the frustrations and moments of utter despair and the unlikeliness of ever making it to publication, she loved sitting down in front of the computer and losing herself in her world.

She wandered out into the soft limpid air of early morning and looked around the garden and the sea, her eyes filling with tears that held something of delight, something of sorrow.

Leaving the man who owned all this beauty would tear her heart to shreds, yet she couldn't wish that things were different; however painful the loss, she could only be grateful that she'd met Paul.

That week, as summer dreamed its way towards Christmas, Jacinta wrote and dreamed with it. She was even cautiously pleased with what she'd written, although by now she was beginning to realise that this book might never be published. This one was her primer; it was teaching her how to weave together all the threads that eventually linked tightly into a novel.

She read and reread the book Paul had bought her, finding something new and useful every time. And each time she picked it up it was with secret delight because he'd been thoughtful enough to think of her. It was a pathetic little flame of pleasure to warm herself at, but she hugged it to her.

The week he'd planned to be away dragged into ten days. Jacinta tried not to think of him. She was reasonably successful while she was awake, but when she slept her unconscious took over, and she was plagued by dreams that ranged perilously close to nightmares, dreams where he turned away from her, dreams where Meriam Anderson threw mud at her sari, and tore the veil...

Dreams that were pitifully simple to understand.

'He's coming back on the weekend,' Fran said one evening. 'His office in Auckland rang—he's on his way back from Europe, but he's decided to stay a couple of days over in Los Angeles.'

Where Meriam Anderson lived.

Jealousy, Jacinta thought, trying hard to be objective,

was a strange thing. She had no right to be jealous; Paul had given her no reason to hope. He'd been kind—but then, he was that sort of man. He was kind to Fran, to Dean, he'd been kind to her mother.

And she despised jealousy. Yet there it was, hot and sullen as embers, casting its lurid glow over her life.

'Use it as raw material for Mage in the book,' she told herself, half seriously. It certainly gave her a much better idea of the agony she was putting her hero through, but it made her feel a parasite on her own emotions.

Walking it off with long treks around the coast and across the hills, often accompanied by one of the farm dogs that had grown too old for hard work, did help; she enjoyed Floss's company, and that too was new to her. Her mother had always had cats.

The evening before Paul was due home Fran went out to dinner, so Jacinta made a salad of crisp, frilly red and green lettuce with avocado, cooked some tiny, white-skinned potatoes and the first of the beans, and poached a new-laid egg. She ate it all, but it could just as well have been seaweed for any enjoyment she got from it.

The evenings were drawing out, and in spite of showers that had freshened the garden it was still unseasonably hot. During the afternoon Jacinta had printed out her whole manuscript, and when she'd eaten she took the pages onto the verandah to read.

But after a while she sat motionless as the dusk drifted down around her, appreciating the silent, lush beauty of the garden and the patient, soft murmur of the sea. The light grew thicker, more golden, distilling pure colour from each flower and summoning a loitering sweetness so that the garden glowed with a fragrant, beckoning glamour.

An unknown hunger ached through her bones, filling her with a seeking, rapturous discontent. Anchoring the manuscript with a smooth stone she'd picked up from the beach, she got to her feet and walked out into the radiance; she hadn't bothered to do up her hair after her swim, and she shook it around her shoulders, at once oppressed by its weight and yet enjoying the freedom.

She reached to pull down a rose whose petals blended shades of apricot and gold and pink, burying her nose in the heart to wallow in perfume. Sinful, she thought, breathing it deeply; that scent was both an invitation and a satisfaction, tantalising yet not complete, because it lured another response from deep inside her, a primitive yearning that consumed her.

A movement on the edge of her vision brought her head around; in the pool of darkness beneath the verandah roof stood a darker figure, a figure she'd invoked from the furthest reaches of desire.

And then he walked down the steps, and the last of the sun caught his fair head, turning it suddenly into gold. Jacinta's hand clenched on the stem beneath the rose, and a thorn caught beside her nail, tearing the sensitive flesh. An involuntary whimper broke from her lips.

'What is it?' Paul asked, his stride lengthening.

Mutely she held out her hand.

He took it gently. 'Old Abraham Darby has some fierce thorns,' he said, and lifted her hand and took her finger into his mouth.

Sensation, fierce as wildfire, robbed Jacinta of volition. She felt her eyes dilate as he sucked the little wound before examining it with frowning absorption, and she prayed that he wouldn't notice her quiver when he ran his thumb across her suddenly sensitive palm.

'It should be all right,' he said. 'You smell of the flower.' He leaned across her to snap off the heavy bloom and gave it to her. 'Some small recompense.'

'I didn't think you were coming back until tomorrow,' she said. Her voice was a little thin, but without any noticeable tremors.

'I was, but things changed.'

'Fran's having dinner with friends.'

Dusk was falling swiftly, the dampness of the air intensifying the mingled scents around them—the clean fresh perfume of the grass, the salty tang of the sea, and the erotic perfume of rose and gardenia and bouvardia.

'Is she?' He sounded slightly tense.

Get a grip on yourself, Jacinta commanded. She took what she hoped seemed a casual step away from his suffocating presence and asked, 'Have you had dinner? There's salad—'

'I'm not hungry; they practically force-feed you on planes.' He wasn't curt but she could hear impatience behind the words.

Turned away from the painful pleasure of looking at him, she began to walk back towards the house. He went with her, saying, 'I'm going to make myself a drink. Would you like one?'

Perhaps a cup of tea would calm her down. 'Yes, thank you,' she said. 'I've got some stuff out on the verandah that might get damp so I'll put it away first.'

She was shivering when she got back to the lounger. After staring at the rose in her hand, she thrust it into the buttonhole of her shirt and gathered up the sheaf of paper with no regard for tidiness or order. Her mind drummed with one thought.

Get out of here before it's too late.

But her heart whispered that it was already too late. Out in the sumptuous beauty of the garden, she had taken a step through a forbidden door and into a different world.

Closing her eyes, she took a deep breath and then another, but neither that nor concentration quenched the slow burn of desire. In fact her head spun slightly, and she thought, You're hyperventilating, for heaven's sake!

Cold water would remove that hectic flush from her skin, and might just shock her system back into normality. But when she went out into the hall Paul said from the far end, 'Your drink's ready.'

Oddly intimidated by the way he watched her, by his

stillness, she walked towards him. He hadn't made tea; the tray he carried held a decanter and bottles.

'Open the door, will you?' he asked, the deep, cool voice without expression.

She did so, and went ahead of him into the conservatory where the frangipani held its cream and gold flowers up in huge panicles. Behind the hills to the west, the sky glowed scarlet and gold and a glaring orange.

'Red sky at night, shepherd's delight,' Jacinta said, because she couldn't think of anything else and she had to break that silence. 'Dean's going to be disappointed.'

Paul waited until she'd sat down before asking, 'I gather it hasn't rained.'

'Several showers, but not enough. Dean says you haven't enough grass to see the stock through if this turns out to be a dry summer.'

'The long-range forecast says it will be a dry summer.'

She put down untasted the glass of lime and soda he'd given her; she didn't trust herself to carry it to her lips without spilling it. 'What will you do?'

She'd exchange a few meaningless pleasantries with him and then make an excuse and go to bed. She could control the fizzing excitement in her blood for that long. She wouldn't make a fool of herself.

'We've already started to sell stock,' he said. 'And we have dams and springs—we should come through in a reasonably good state unless it doesn't rain until next May. How's your finger?'

He hadn't turned the light on and the burning sky edged his profile with flames.

'It's all right,' she said vaguely, steadying her hand to reach for her glass. She downed half the cold liquid, and hiccuped.

Paul lifted his glass to his lips. He didn't drink much. 'What's been happening while I've been gone?'

'Nothing much,' she said. It sounded a little bleak, so she added, 'Well, not a lot. I found a seagull on the beach with a broken wing, and Fran and I have been looking after it…' Her voice died away. After a moment, she asked, 'Did your trip go well?'

'Very well.' He almost drawled the words.

Had he seen Meriam Anderson in Los Angeles?

'I've got something for you from Laurence Perry,' he said, answering her unspoken question.

Her heart shivered within her. 'Really?' she said politely.

He took an envelope from his pocket and handed it over. Jacinta opened it and looked down at the print, blinking at the woman curled in voluptuous abandon amongst a huddle of gold and orange and rust, arms and neck gleaming in the torrid light of summer, a veil covering hair the same colour as Jacinta's. Essentially naked beneath the orange veiling, the model slept in front of a shimmering sea.

'Good heavens!' Jacinta said.

'What is it?' Paul spoke softly, yet such was the implicit authority in his tone that she handed the print across to him.

'Ah,' he said after a quick survey. 'High Victoriana. One of Lord Leighton's mock-classical affairs, I'd say.'

The sun dipped beneath the horizon and the afterglow— echoing the colours in the print—throbbed for several seconds before beginning to fade into night's serene dimness.

'Laurence thought I looked like her,' Jacinta said, 'but it was just my ginger hair and the colour and draping of the sari.'

'No, there's a definite resemblance.' Paul's gaze moved slowly, deliberately across her face. 'The colouring, of course, and that straight, very English nose. And the innocent mouth. Judging by the pose and the clothing, I imagine the artist intended that innocence to be deceptive.'

Jacinta ignored the cynical note. 'It was sweet of Laurence to track it down for me.'

'He's a nice man. And he thought you were charming.'

He spoke without expression, yet when he went on pleasantly, 'But then, most people are kind to you, it seems,' she felt the hairs on the back of her neck lift.

To give herself time to cast about for another, less contentious thing to talk about, she picked up her glass and sipped more of the lime and soda, circumspectly this time.

Setting the print down beside a small parcel on the sidetable, he asked, 'How's the book coming along?'

'I'm writing,' she said cautiously. 'It's more fun now that I'm not sticking so closely to a prescribed storyline, but it's much more scary, and it takes longer. I'll have a better idea of where I'm going with the next one.'

'So there's going to be a next one?'

'I—well, yes, I think so.'

'Where are you planning to send this one?'

'I haven't thought yet. I'll have to do some research.'

He picked up the parcel from the table. 'This might help.'

Although it was wrapped, Jacinta could tell by both look and feel that it was another book. Gripping it in her lap, she stammered, 'You're very kind, but really you shouldn't be buying me books, though I've read the last one so often I just about know it off by heart.'

'This one isn't a how-to—it's a listing of publishers and what they're looking for.'

'Thank you,' she said again, looking down at the packet on her lap. Lamely she added, 'I'm sure it will be very helpful.'

'I hope so,' he said negligently.

The darkness in the room gathered, seemed to thicken. Jacinta's pulses thrummed so loudly she thought he must be able to hear them. She unwrapped the book, very aware of Paul leaning back in the chair, as though the trip had sapped even his vitality, long legs stretched out in front of him, the glass he'd barely touched turning slowly in his fingers.

Mesmerised, she watched the tiny flashes from the heart

of the crystal. Her gaze wandered up from the glass to his face, shadowed now, and the pale blur of his hair. Something deep and terrifying blossomed within her, growing to fullness in a second. The door to that different destiny, the world of love, clanged shut behind her, sealing her off from the old familiar life, changing her with inescapable relentlessness.

This, she thought suddenly, is not just love; Paul is the only man I'll ever love like this.

The very banality of the words emphasised them, gave them weight and purpose. Until that moment she'd been playing with the idea of love and passion, skirting it with ambivalence, but between one second and the next she knew that for her there would be no other love.

And even as she shrank back—because if Paul was the only man for her then she'd always be alone—she accepted the bitter knowledge. Her mother had loved her father until she died; his name had been on her lips as she drew her last breath.

For the first time she understood—and understood, too, why her mother had always said that having a daughter had been the one thing that went right in her life. If she could have Paul's child she would love it and care for it...

But for her there would be no child. And that was a burden, a grief she couldn't deal with now, not when the shock of discovery was still piercing her heart.

She waited until she'd regained the control she needed to say with a careful, remote precision, 'You must be tired. I am too, so I'll head for bed now.'

'Goodnight.' He got to his feet as she did, and stood aside courteously, then bent and picked up the print Laurence had found for her. 'You'd better take this,' he said, holding it out.

She took it, but her hand was shaking and their fingers touched.

Paul said between his teeth, 'Damn, damn, *damn*,' and

the vivid scrap of paper fell unnoticed to the floor as he pulled Jacinta into his arms.

Yes, she thought exultantly, and with mindless hunger she tilted her face. When he bent his head and took her seeking mouth she met his kiss like a flame.

Heat raged through her, setting her alight until she thought she could feel sparks shooting from her skin. But when his mouth crushed hers the quality of her response altered. Just as intense, just as cataclysmic, sensation ran slow and lazy and languorous through her, melting her bones and seducing open the gates of her will-power.

Lifting his head, he said thickly, 'Jacinta, I've wanted you ever since I saw you. In Fiji I couldn't sleep for wondering what your pretty mouth would feel like under mine...'

Dazzled, she sighed, and he took what he wanted, filling her with his taste, male, dark and mysterious, overwhelming her with expertise, summoning her hidden wildness in response to his passionate mastery.

When at last the kiss ended they were both breathing erratically, and he surveyed her tender mouth with eyes that were narrowed and lit from within, purposeful and determined on conquest.

Desire clutched at her heart; everything inside her deliquesced, to be remade anew by that intent gaze. In a soft, tentative voice she said his name, loving the sound of it on her lips, shaping her mouth to his liking, to her need.

'Paul,' she breathed again, fascinated by the blue fire that ringed the dilating blackness at the centre of his eyes.

Once more she readied her mouth for his erotic plunder, but this time he kissed beneath her ear, and while he showed her how fiercely sensitive that spot was his hands slid up into her hair and he pulled her head back gently, so that he could kiss her jaw, and the corner of her mouth, then down the length of her throat to the throbbing hollow at its base.

Racked by delight, she trembled. An inarticulate murmur broke helplessly from her throat, and he smiled.

God, she thought, appalled for a sane moment by her happiness, what pleasure to feel this man's smile against my skin!

His hands lingered through her hair until she moaned with the pleasure of it, then skimmed her shoulders, and it was no longer happiness she felt, but something thunderous and uncontrollable, a compulsion that demanded satisfaction.

'Jacinta,' he said, his voice impeded and oddly hesitant as he took the crushed rose from her buttonhole and dropped it. 'So sweet and summery and fragrant. What was it Shakespeare asked? ''Shall I compare thee to a summer's day? Thou art more lovely and more temperate.''' His laughter was husky, almost raw. 'Certainly more lovely, but I think he might have got the temperate part wrong, thank God.'

Afterwards she'd think that he'd wielded the instrument of his voice like a weapon, disarming her completely, but at the time she could only respond helplessly to its magnetism.

And then his fingers cupped her breasts. Jacinta shivered, and her head fell back, and the strength seeped from her.

Slowly, murmuring his appreciation, he slipped open the buttons down the front of her shirt, the swift, sure movements of his fingers a delicious torment. Lifting weighted eyelids, she watched the concentration in his face and the pulse flicking in his jaw, and knew that whatever happened she was not going to regret this.

The calm good humour was gone; it had only ever been a mask that hid the hunter, the predator, from the eyes of the world. This man knew what he was doing, held his goal firmly in mind.

And yet she wasn't afraid, for this was Paul and she loved him. Although fierce determination sculpted his face, she knew intuitively that he wouldn't be brutal, or exploit her untutored ardour. He would take, yes, but he would give in equal measure.

So when the front of her shirt fell open and he unclasped her bra and pushed both shirt and bra down her arms, she shrugged free of the cloth and lifted her arms and put them around his neck.

'Not so quickly,' he said, eyes kindling. 'Let me look at you.'

That was harder to deal with; she felt the track of his gaze across pale skin and to her astonishment the apricot centres of her breasts stiffened and sprang forth, and he laughed softly. Before she realised what he was going to do he bent and took one in his mouth while moving a thumb smoothly, persistently over the other.

She knew the mechanics of lovemaking. But no one had ever warned her that such gentle suckling could kindle lightning in her cells. Shuddering, fighting to keep her lashes from drifting down, she looked at the golden head against her breast and felt her womb contract in a fierce, involuntary spasm.

'Paul,' she said soundlessly, but he heard her and straightened, that splintering fire incandescent now around the dark pupils of his eyes.

'Yes,' he said, and this time there was no sweet summer wooing in his words, nothing but a stripped desperation that was infinitely more exciting.

Jacinta gasped when he picked her up. Cradled by iron muscles, made speechless by the sheer primitive force of his actions, she said, 'I'm too heavy!'

'No,' he said harshly, 'just right for me.' And certainly he showed no signs of strain as he carried her down the hallway.

His bedroom door was ajar; he kicked it wide and went through, shouldering it closed behind him, and walked across the shadowy room to put her on her feet beside a big, four-poster bed.

Jacinta stumbled slightly, and wailed, 'I'm so clumsy,' when he grabbed her and supported her.

'You're not,' he said, his voice soothing yet shot through with a turbulent rasp that fired her blood anew. 'Don't worry.'

She stared up into eyes so blue and so blazing she thought they scorched her skin. 'I'm not,' she whispered. 'Worrying, I mean.'

Laughter glinted a moment in the sapphire depths. 'Then would you like to undress me?' he asked gravely. 'I've spent a lot of time imagining how your hands would feel on me.'

Until that moment she'd always assumed that making love was something a man did to a woman. Now, dazzled by the idea of sharing, she nodded, and undid the buttons on his shirt. Tentatively she spread her hands over his heart, feeling the silky abrasion of hair against her palms, the unsteady, driving pulse.

I'm doing that to him, she thought, awed, flexing fingers until he startled her with a muffled groan. Eyes widening, she looked up. Although his mouth was controlled into a straight line, the contours were slightly swollen, and in the severe features she saw a stark hunger that matched hers. It should have frightened her but she wasn't afraid. The secret pathways in her body moistened, heated.

'You're so strong,' she murmured, surprising herself.

'Is that what you like? Strength?'

Her hands slid beneath the fine material of his shirt to find the smooth swell of muscle along his shoulders, the sleekness of his skin only emphasising the male power hidden beneath it.

'I suppose I do.' Her voice was rich and full. 'And beauty.' She laughed a little in her throat. 'And you are beautiful.'

Amazingly, colour patched along the broad sweep of his cheekbones. 'So are you,' he said, shucking off his shirt.

'You don't have to say that.'

He looked at her, his brows drawing together. 'I don't lie,' he said, and kissed the place where her neck joined her shoulder, pulling a strand of hair over so that it curled down to meet the curve of her breast.

'You light the night sky,' he said, and this time she knew he meant it. His voice was implacable, almost fierce, and his hand moved slowly down to cup her breast again, the long fingers dark against the pale ivory of her skin.

'All fire and light and heat, like flames in a dreary world,' he said, and kissed her, his mouth hard and ravenous, as though he couldn't get enough of her.

After that she followed where he led, a novice in the hands of a master, until at last she lay naked before him.

'Flames everywhere,' he said. When she blushed he smiled, the lazy, sexy smile of a man who knew that he was going to get what he wanted, and startled her by kissing her hipbone.

His mouth was warm and persuasive, and she had to remember to breathe, to drag air into parched lungs, because everything she'd taken for granted about her body over the years was now shown to be false.

Paul stood up and shed the rest of his clothes without ceremony, then came down beside her on the bed, slipping an arm under her head.

She lifted a solemn face and met the hard, consuming passion of his gaze. In his throat the pulse hammered rapidly. Jacinta rested her index finger on that small betrayal, then traced down the midline of his chest to one narrow hip and on to the powerful muscles of his thigh.

She didn't touch the thrusting jut of his masculinity, but her body softened, opened, readied itself for him. His hand found her mount of Venus, pressing against nerve-endings that sent their dangerous summons throughout every cell in her body.

One finger gently separated her hidden folds; his mouth was still straight and firmly closed, his eyes masked by dark lashes.

Fire danced through her at the touch of his fingers, soon augmented by a conflagration that overpowered her, a remorseless, building, honeyed sweetness of wanting, an unmeasured compulsion that set the wildness in her free, so that she gasped his name and arced towards him, pulling him down, her hips moving erotically beneath him, her face absorbed and demanding.

Making love with Paul meant surrendering to her own desires so that the focus of her world narrowed to this bed, this man; nothing else mattered. Entirely lost in the sensuous overload, Jacinta spun into a region beyond time and place—a region where she and he were all that existed.

Slowly, skilfully, he brought her to such readiness that her hand on his skin shook, and she shivered and pressed herself against him, eagerly supplicant. Then, at last, he took her, sliding into the passage he'd prepared, both of them so still that the only movement was the tightening muscles in his haunches as he pushed into her.

Jacinta surged suddenly upwards, enclosing him and surrounding him, and the muscles in her legs gripped and held in the same primeval clasp as her secret, inner muscles.

'Yes,' he said, and took her breath away by driving home, and without waiting withdrawing and thrusting again, setting up an erotic rhythm that she soon picked up, meeting each thrust with an answering twist of her hips, her hands clenched across the expanse of his back as the muscles bunched and knotted and she went with him down that long, ravishing path to fulfilment.

At some stage she understood dimly that he was restraining himself, making sure he didn't climax before she reached her peak, and although she loved him for his consideration she didn't want that. She wanted him as lost in this wonderful experience as she was, unable to think of anything other than this miracle.

Excitement began to soar beyond rational thought; sensation, rich and multifarious, flooded her. She grasped his lean hips and held him there while she moved against him, and when his heavy eyelids lifted she smiled and drowned in blueness as wave after wave tossed her higher and higher beyond some impalpable barrier where she was nothing but feeling, so consumed by ecstasy that she cried out as her body shuddered beneath his.

And then he clamped her hips in his callused hands and went with her into that place where nothing else existed but the two of them. For long moments they remained wrapped in each other's arms while the aftershocks of orgasm buffeted through them, leaving them slick with sweat that cooled slowly, yet faster than desire and passion.

When at last he pushed himself up on his elbows she gave an inarticulate murmur of protest and opened sated, drowsy eyes. He looked, she thought with a jolt of the heart, strained, although he smiled and bent to kiss her mouth gently.

'It's all right,' he said, turning onto his side so that she could breathe more easily. He didn't loosen his grip.

After a while she realised that he'd gone to sleep, and outrage warred with amusement.

It somehow made him seem much more—human—and she had to admit that she was tired too.

And more than content to stay where she was.

Oddly enough, just before she drifted off to sleep, her last, barely conscious thought was that she was glad his jilting Aura had never been in this house.

Jacinta woke hours later, to complete bewilderment. A soft light shone through the uncurtained windows, but she wasn't in her own room—and then, as her night-accustomed eyes roamed the room, she remembered.

Fully-clothed, Paul was standing in the window. Suddenly racked by embarrassment at her nudity under the sheet, she said uncertainly, 'Paul?'

'I'm here.'

'I know.' Her fingers plucked nervously at the sheet.

'What—?' The words wouldn't come. She swallowed, and started again. 'What are you doing?'

'Wondering how I'm going to tell my cousin that I've broken his trust and slept with the woman he's engaged to.' He spoke with grim distinctness, every word an arrow directed at himself as well as her.

CHAPTER EIGHT

PAUL'S words hummed and buzzed in her ears, echoing so that she couldn't make sense of them. Secret, inchoate dreams she'd been building in her unconscious mind shrivelled into dust, doomed before she'd even recognised them.

'What?' she asked.

He didn't turn, but the light of dawn caught on his hair. 'You heard me,' he said evenly.

Jacinta forced herself to speak with slow, painstaking care. 'I *thought* I heard you. Where the *hell* did you get that idea?'

'From Gerard, of course,' he said, scorn icing the words. 'He told me when he arranged for you to stay here.'

She drew in a deep, ragged breath and sat up, arms folded across her breasts to hold the sheet in place. Her hair fell across her shoulders, slippery and warm. If she let herself, she'd remember the way his hands had speared through it...

'I don't believe this,' she said, trying to sound reasonable and sensible. 'Gerard wouldn't have told you that because he knows it's not true.'

'He said that you'd kept it secret because universities don't welcome affairs between tutors and students. It makes sense.' His voice was studied and dispassionate, as though they'd never lain together locked in the most intimate embrace of all, breasts crushed against chest, legs intertwined, mouth to mouth, open to each other.

She shook her head, seizing on what seemed to her chaotic mind to be the flaw in his argument. 'I'm not his student now.'

'True, but he's going to be your supervisor next year.' Although he didn't move, she shivered at the icy condemnation in his tone.

He was serious. Or was this a perverted sort of kiss-off?

She said heavily, 'Do you honestly think that I'd be—here—if I was secretly engaged to Gerard?'

'It depends on why you're engaged to him,' he said almost indifferently. 'If it's because you want security, then, yes, you might well feel that I'm a better bet than he is. I don't blame you for that—your childhood must have been lacking in stability.'

'That's big of you,' she said between her teeth. 'As it happens, you're quite wrong. My mother kept me fed and loved, and that's the sort of stability most children need.' A sudden memory narrowed her eyes. 'I suppose you thought I was eyeing up Dean and Laurence Perry too, seeing which one offered the most *stability*.'

'It seemed possible,' he said stonily.

Pain began to niggle behind her eyes. 'I must be extraordinarily stupid. That's why you kept bringing Dean's Brenda into the conversation.'

'It doesn't matter. What does matter is Gerard.'

'I don't believe this.' Exhaustion numbed her mind, making it impossible to follow her fleeting fragments of thought to a logical conclusion. Ignoring the sheet, she pressed the heels of her hands to her eyes and strove desperately for composure.

Eventually she was able to say woodenly, 'He's never touched me. Never. Not even a kiss.' She paused, but Paul said nothing, didn't move. A wild mixture of emotions clogged her throat. 'If I'd thought he was in love with me I wouldn't have accepted the computer, or worked for him—'

'Or let him subsidise your accommodation?' Paul interpolated smoothly.

Jacinta's head came up. 'What?' she croaked.

In a clipped, metallic voice he said, 'He subsidises your rent at the flat—the flat he found for you—by fifty dollars a week. He plans to pay out more for your tuition fees next year.'

'He said he knew of a grant,' she said hesitantly. 'For women whose tertiary education has been interrupted by family concerns. It's given out by a trust.'

'Gerard's trust.' He didn't try to hide the scorn that blazed through his words. Inexorably he went on, 'And the flat? Did you really believe his tale of someone who was in Oxford on a scholarship?'

'I had no reason not to,' she cried out, realising for the first time how naïve she'd been.

'It didn't occur to you,' he drawled, 'that to accept the offer of accommodation from a man who was sexually interested in you—'

She leapt out of the bed and flew across to him, hand upraised. 'He wasn't— I didn't—oh!'

For he'd caught her hand and twisted it behind her back, not painfully but with relentless speed, bringing her up against him. He was wearing a cotton robe in some dark material, thin enough to reveal his arousal.

Her breath stopping in her lungs, Jacinta registered the sharp aroma of danger. Her rage ebbed into humiliation as she stared into his implacable eyes, and she shivered, the cool morning air flowing through the open window and over her naked body.

'Don't ever hit me,' Paul said, his voice so soft she barely heard it, yet each word resounded through her head. He was holding onto his control with the thinnest of reins, and for the first time in her life Jacinta was truly afraid of a man.

Gerard had bragged that his cousin never lost his temper, that no one had ever seen him angry. Gerard had been wrong.

That icy, concentrated contempt terrified her.

'Why would he do all that for you if he didn't plan to marry you? He's never been the sort of man who resorts to prostitutes, and he's too intelligent to pay out for a woman with a prostitute's mind. He's been helping the woman he loves, the woman he plans to marry.'

Her hold on reality slipping, she closed her eyes. 'No,' she whispered.

'I've known my cousin for as long as he's lived, and he's not a liar.'

'He lied to both of us,' she shot back on a surge of adrenalin. And because she couldn't surrender to the despair that threatened to exhaust her, she whipped up her anger to add savagely, 'Unless he felt that lying was the only way he could protect me from you.'

His features clamped into an impervious mask. 'If so, it didn't work,' he said, coldly sardonic. 'And if he thought you needed protection from me, that still implies a much closer relationship than you're admitting to. A man is only so protective of the woman he calls his.'

Jacinta jerked her arm, and he released her as though she fouled his hands. Hot denials hovered on her tongue, but she could see from his bleak, uncompromising face that nothing she could say would convince him that Gerard had lied.

Accepting that it was useless, she turned away and drew in a long, agonising breath while she struggled for the strength to get her through the next few minutes.

'For God's sake put some clothes on,' Paul said between his teeth.

Shame and embarrassment roiled over her. She walked quickly back to the small pile of her clothes on the floor and began to get into them.

It didn't help that she understood. Aura had run away with Paul's best friend; he had just spent the night with the woman he believed to be engaged to his cousin. Not only did he despise Jacinta, he despised himself.

Steadily she said, 'Men don't own women.'

He smiled, and a shiver ran down her spine. 'Tell that to a jealous lover.'

'I'm not going to debate that,' she said fiercely, yanking on her shorts. 'You know it's wrong. No one has the right to own anyone else. As for Gerard, he lied.'

'So you say.'

She swallowed, knowing it was hopeless to protest her innocence. He believed his cousin.

And that, she thought painfully, was an even greater betrayal than his physical rejection of her.

Without bothering to put on her bra, she shrugged into the shirt and began to fasten the buttons, concentrating fiercely on the mundane task because it was all she had to keep the demons of despair at bay.

'Unfortunately,' he said, 'I'll have to tell him.'

'It's none of his business,' she said, but without conviction.

The quotation from Shakespeare was burnt in letters of fire across her brain, along with the one he'd murmured to her the preceding evening. She'd never, she thought savagely, be able to read Shakespeare again without having both scenes, last night and this morning, spring to life again.

Mine honour is my life; both grow in one
Take honour from me, and my life is done.

A dangerous honour, she thought bitterly.

A swift glance revealed Paul's austere, ruthless profile against the light of the day outside; she thought of Vikings, of men who held to their conscience in the face of death. Because he hated himself for betraying his cousin's trust, he was putting them both through the rigorous hell he assigned to violators of his code.

He said, 'I can't let him marry you knowing that we—'

'Wanted each other? Slept together?' She scooped up

her sandals and headed towards the door. 'Don't spoil your relationship with Gerard over me,' she threw over her shoulder. 'I'm not going to marry him, or sleep with him, ever. Whatever relationship he's implied is a product of his imagination and exists only in his head. He needs a psychiatrist.'

It wasn't a very satisfying parting shot but it was all she could think of. Back in her room she sat down on the bed and tried to reassemble her thoughts, but after a moment her sandals and underwear dropped from limp fingers and she gave in to the luxury of tears, curling up in a ball on the bedcover while she wept.

It was the sudden transition from heaven to hell, she thought drearily, the abrupt and shattering destruction of all her illusions.

Perhaps she'd deserved to have them destroyed. She'd been utterly credulous.

Shame dried the tears. Why had Gerard lied? Why, when she wouldn't accept money from him, had he come up with this elaborate deception—helped, of course, by her gullibility?

Simple kindness was no answer. Had he truly fantasised that her acceptance of his help meant that she was falling in love with him? Surely he didn't plan to reveal the amount she owed him and suggest the oldest way in the world to repay it?

Jacinta got up and walked across to the window. Several blackbirds immediately shrieked a warning from the lawn and flew low and straight into the garden border.

He was sick, or he was like Mark, who fed a shaky ego on women's vulnerability. And she'd fallen for it. Was there something in her that signalled to men that she was a fool?

She owed Gerard money she wasn't going to be able to repay. Unless she used her mother's money.

'Oh, Mum,' she whispered thickly, resting her head against the cool glass.

She stayed like that until the sun bounded up over the edge of the sea. Then, exhausted and aching, she collected clean clothes together and went to the bathroom.

As she dried herself in front of the big mirror she looked gravely at the soft red marks on her breasts with a heavy-lidded, sated gaze that the morning's events hadn't been able to banish.

Paul had tempered his great strength until his control had snapped. And even then he hadn't hurt her; her skin was fine and easily bruised.

A wave of erotic longing gathered in the pit of her stomach. As an initiation into the delights of making love—sex, she corrected—hers had been wonderful. Perhaps Paul had been born knowing how to bring a woman to the heights of ecstasy, but experience had refined that initial understanding to a skilled, passionate mastery that overwhelmed her.

Yet in some basic way he mistrusted all women.

Because of the woman who'd left him to run away with his best friend? It was too easy, too pat. Other men had endured similar experiences yet learned to trust again.

Her mother used to say 'Look to the child' when they discussed the foibles of friends and neighbours. Probably the root cause of Paul's mistrust, of his rigid insistence on honour, lay buried deep in his childhood.

While she'd showered her unconscious had made her decision for her. She'd give up her university studies and find a job, using her mother's legacy to reimburse Gerard.

Back in her room she began to pack, biting her lip to hold in the tears until she managed to achieve a measure of self-control.

A knock on the door made her freeze, her breath solid-ifying in a hard lump at the centre of her chest.

Don't be silly, she told herself as she went across to open it. He won't hurt you.

Paul stood outside, his expression remote and guarded. 'We have to talk,' he said. His eyes, their blueness leached of emotion and warmth, focused on the suitcase at the side of the bed. 'But not now. Jacinta, there's an emergency at sea—a boat's on fire—and I'm going out with Dean in a spotter plane from the Aero Club. Wait here until I get back. And don't make any arrangements until you hear what I have to say.'

A hidden, fugitive hope persuaded her to say, 'All right.'

He nodded. 'Thank you,' he said, meticulously polite as ever, and turned and strode down the hall towards his room.

It was a long morning. After Jacinta had finished packing she went into the kitchen and forced down toast and coffee.

Fran said, 'That's not going to keep you going for long.'

'It's enough. Why are Dean and Paul searching for a boat that's on fire?'

'Because the idiot has no idea where he is,' Fran said shortly. 'He radioed in to the coastguard, but he's out of sight of land so he's lost.'

Aren't we all? Jacinta thought cynically.

Still cocooned in a merciful numbness, she cleared everything from the computer so that no one would be able to read her manuscript, and put the two sets of diskettes into her suitcase.

At morning tea Jacinta surrendered to her driving curiosity and asked Fran as casually as she could, 'How long have you worked for Paul?'

'Five years; since my marriage broke up,' the housekeeper told her readily. 'But my dad used to work for his parents, so I've known him all my life. He was a lovely boy: a bit serious and always very responsible, and that smile of his—well, you know what it's like.'

Once she'd left Waitapu she'd never see that smile again. Jacinta said, 'His parents are both dead, aren't they?'

'Yes. His father was a hard man and you didn't cross him—everyone liked him as well as respected him, though.

He was a good man. A bit like Paul, really, without the charm. Paul got that from his mother. She was lovely, but she was sort of distant, as though she didn't really live in this world. I don't think she knew how to deal with children.' Fran glanced out of the window. 'Yes,' she said, 'I thought we might have rain today. Look at that front coming up.'

By lunchtime it was raining properly. Jacinta couldn't eat anything, and she couldn't settle either. Was that distant mother the clue to Paul's character? A hard father and a distant, charming mother...

Fran, who'd apparently been keeping an eye on her, came into the morning room as she put down a book, and said, 'Why don't you watch a video?'

'I suppose I could.' Perhaps a video would help keep the gnawing agony at bay. She might be able to lose herself in a good story.

'There's a stack of them in the bottom left-hand cupboard there, underneath the bookshelves,' Fran said.

The books in the morning room were the sort kept to entertain visitors—local history and geology, books by New Zealanders. Paul's main collection was kept in his office, into which Jacinta had never even looked, let alone stepped. He also read magazines of all sorts: literary, science, farming, and manufacturing and business. Jacinta had enjoyed herself with the contents of the morning room bookshelves, but she'd never bothered with the videos.

They turned out to be an interesting selection. Several classics, some very good dramas, a few comedies, and items that had been taped from the television, most labelled in a strong hand.

Fascinated, because these were programmes Paul had wanted to watch, Jacinta sat through a hard-hitting political discussion recorded a few months previously, a programme on a small New Zealand town she remembered seeing some years ago with her mother, and what appeared to be an amateur video of a pastoral show.

Halfway through that it switched to a few minutes of a party that someone had filmed on a camcorder. Jacinta didn't know anyone until the camera swivelled, and there was Paul. A younger Paul, somehow more—more lightweight than the man she knew. As the camera fixed onto him he smiled, and that smile was heartbreakingly familiar, warm and lazy and sweet.

He was smiling at the woman beside him. Jacinta drew in an anguished breath as she scrutinised the beautiful, passionate face beneath hair that glowed like burgundy. 'A dark flame', Gerard had called her.

This was Aura, who'd run away with Paul's best friend.

Jacinta sat very still while the man who'd been taking the video called out, 'Smile for me, Aura,' and, sure enough, the woman smiled.

Something tore inside Jacinta. How could she even think of comparing herself to such beauty?

Scarcely knowing what she did, she stopped the video, rewound it to play those fleeting moments over in excruciating detail.

Aura looked at Paul with loving affection, with pleasure and friendliness, but there was nothing in those wonderful eyes that came close to the feelings Jacinta had for him.

She was watching the couple turn away from the camera to talk to an elderly woman when a lethal voice said behind her, 'Turn that bloody thing off.'

Terror kicking in her stomach, Jacinta twisted. Paul stood just inside the door, his eyes the searing blue at the heart of a diamond, a white line around his mouth.

The hubbub of the party was cut abruptly short, replaced by the unctuous voice of a television front-man announcing another documentary.

'Turn it off,' Paul repeated, his voice as cold and violent as an Arctic storm.

Jacinta had to force herself to press the switch on the remote so that the picture was swallowed up in blackness.

Self-protection drove her stiffly to her feet. 'Did you find the boat?'

At first she thought he wasn't going to answer, but after a taut couple of seconds he said, 'Yes. Where the hell did you get that video?'

Refusing to let her hands clench at her side, she said, 'It's just a fragment. I was watching a documentary you'd taped, and it appeared between it and the next thing you taped.' She bit her lip to stop the babbling words.

'I see.' Leashed by superhuman control, his anger was replaced by a frigid detachment that was even more forbidding. Apparently thinking she needed some sort of explanation, he said, 'It's old—over five years old.'

And he turned. He was, she realised, going to leave it at that.

She said, 'It still hurts, doesn't it?'

'No.'

'Then why did you react so aggressively?'

'Jacinta, stop it.' He sounded tired.

Oh, God, she wanted to. If she could wipe the impressions of the last ten minutes from her brain she'd do it—and even as the thought was born she knew she lied. There could be no peace for her without the truth. She waited, her eyes fixed on his handsome face.

'I loved her once,' he said impatiently, frowning. 'It's over now—has been for years.'

'If you no longer love her why do you keep up the feud?'

His eyes narrowed. With silky, unpleasant emphasis he said, 'Gerard's been gossiping, has he? There is no feud. Never has been.'

'So you see them regularly? Aura and her husband.'

Through thin lips he said, 'No.'

'Because you can't bear to.'

'Not at all,' he said with calm, snubbing courtesy. 'I have as little taste as most people for being made to look a fool, so I suppose it's pride that prevents us from being a cosy, friendly trio.'

Jacinta looked at him. Not only the intervening five years had made the difference between the man who stood in front of her now and the Paul McAlpine who'd smiled at Aura with such love and confidence. That man had been—softer? No, that was the wrong word.

Losing the woman had hardened Paul, put an edge to his personality that hadn't been there before. That inborn strength and assurance had been honed by anger and determination into compelling power and authority. Aura's betrayal had turned him into a dominating, almost disturbingly formidable man, intensely attractive to women.

Would Aura have run away with her Flint if she'd truly known this man?

Jacinta said quietly, 'I think you're still in love with her.'

He took a step towards her, but halted when she braced herself. He swore beneath his breath, a curse she couldn't quite hear, then she saw him reimpose control, all emotion transmuted by his iron self-discipline into harsh inflexibility.

'That's quite an assumption to make after seeing a minute of old film,' he said aloofly, watching her with eyes opaque as blue stones.

'It was your reaction that gave you away.' Jacinta tested her courage, found it wanting, yet persisted. 'If you don't love her then you must hate her.'

His handsome features were as unrevealing as granite. 'Far from it,' he said, his calculated politeness hurting Jacinta more than open anger ever could have. 'I wish her every happiness.'

That was when Jacinta accepted that the only thing she could do was leave the homestead and go away and hope that she never saw him again. Even if he told her that he loved her she'd have to go, but he was not, she thought with a trace of bitterness, going to lie to her.

He couldn't love another woman because his heart was buried in Aura's shrine.

'It's none of my business,' she said, scarcely knowing what the words were, falling back on conventional phrases because she could never say what she really felt.

'You're right, it's not. It's long over. What are your plans?'

'I'll go back to Auckland.'

His gaze flicked past her to the window. 'Not in this downpour,' he said.

Shrugging, she said, 'I'll go on the bus. I rang to see if they had a spare seat for this afternoon, and they have. I'll have to ask someone to take me in to the village, if that's all right.'

Speaking slowly, he said, 'If you stay the night here I'll take you back tomorrow morning.'

'It will be much easier if I go tonight.'

'Where are you going?'

Oddly enough, she hadn't thought of that. She stared at her hands, laced tightly together in front of her, and tried to think, but the thoughts were lost in a woolly fog. 'The YWCA,' she finally blurted when the silence had stretched on too long.

'Have you got everything you own packed into those two suitcases?'

Pity she could definitely do without. In a tone that matched his for evenness, she said, 'No, and don't worry about me, Paul, I'll be all right. I may have been very naïve with Gerard, but I'm actually quite competent at managing my life. I'll cope.'

With a twist of his lips, he said brutally, 'How? You've no job—'

'I'll find one.'

'—and very little money. I will worry about you.' He paused, then added stiffly, 'And so will Gerard.'

Anger kindled in her, fast and lethal as a backblast. Lifting her head, she demanded fiercely, 'Do you still believe that I'm engaged to him?'

His expression revealed nothing. 'I don't know,' he said after a prolonged pause. 'One of you is lying. If Gerard lied it would make him psychologically unstable, and I've never seen any evidence of that in him. Whereas I've seen a lot of women who consciously or unconsciously look for security in the man they plan to marry. It's probably inbred in us; men go for beauty, women go for money and status, and I'm sure it's all for the better perpetuation of the species.'

She had no answer to the cynical observation, no defences against him.

He added in a different voice, 'But I'm not going to just drop you at the YWCA and leave you, so you'd better come up with some sort of address to go to.'

Rain drove at the windows, and with the sudden intensity of a summer storm overflowed the gutterings, so that the rest of the world was walled off by a shimmering, liquid tent. To her horror Jacinta's eyes began to fill; hastily she grabbed her handkerchief from her pocket and blew her nose.

I will not cry, she vowed. I will *not*...

Stiffly Paul said, 'Jacinta, you don't have to flee to the YWCA as though you've been thrown out. I'll move back to town until you can find a permanent place to go to. I usually spend this time in Auckland anyway; it's the busiest time of the year because everyone wants every deal settled by Christmas Eve.'

She shook her head. 'It'll be easier on everyone if I go now. This afternoon.'

Unerringly, he chose the one thing that might change her mind. 'It won't be easier on me,' he said coolly. 'Be sensible. Shall we make it a week? You should be able to find somewhere to live in that time, and I'll know you're safe.'

'I'd be perfectly safe at the YWCA,' she pointed out desperately.

'They might not have a room,' he said.

Clearly he was prepared to argue all day until she gave in. She could just go, but she didn't want to use Gerard's car—the thought of driving it down to Auckland made her feel unclean. Someone from Waitapu was going to have to drive her in to catch the bus, and one look at Paul's implacable face told her she wasn't going to get any co-operation from him.

Jacinta gave in. 'All right,' she said, because she was exhausted and he was right; a week would give her a chance to find a new home.

'Of course,' he said, 'I want your promise that you won't run away the moment I get out of the gate.'

She flushed and kept her eyes averted. 'Why should you believe my promise?' she asked. 'You won't believe anything else I tell you.'

'Ah, but you keep promises,' he said smoothly. 'You told me so once.'

She flinched. 'I'm supposed to be engaged to Gerard,' she retorted snidely. 'That's a promise too.'

'If you don't give me your word I'll just have to immobilise his car and let everyone here know that you are not to be let out of the gate until I get back,' he said.

It was so outrageous a statement that she stared at him. The blue eyes were darkly shadowed by his lashes, but there was no amusement in his voice or the grim line of his mouth. He looked like someone about to go into battle—a warrior determined to win, steel-honed with implacable purpose.

He meant it.

'Make me a prisoner?' she asked, tight-lipped.

'If I have to.' His tone gave no quarter.

Jacinta loved him. She had just spent the night making love with him. She would remember him all her life.

But at that moment she could have happily strangled

him. Very steadily she said, 'Threats have a way of re-
bounding on the people who issue them. However, you
don't need to make any more. I'll stay here until I find a
place to go to.'

'Thank you.' He turned, then stopped. Tonelessly he
said, 'I'm sorry.'

'Why?'

'For last night.'

Jacinta had always thought herself placid and even-
tempered, but before he could say any more she interrupted
rapidly, 'I'm not. I enjoyed it immensely. And although
you don't believe me, there was no reason why we
shouldn't have made love. We both wanted it, and neither
of us is responsible for any plans Gerard may have made,
or his attempts to manipulate us.'

He didn't answer directly. Instead he said, 'I'm away
for the afternoon and won't be back until late, so unless
you're up when I leave tomorrow morning, I'll see you in
a week's time.'

She refused to watch him go out of the room, refused
to think of anything but the necessity of getting a place to
live in. Outside the rain stopped and the sun came out,
summoning steam from the paths as it set about drying up
the downpour.

When she heard the car leave she went down the hall
and into her bedroom. Thank God they had slept together
in his bed. This one held no memories.

After a while she fought back the debilitating listless-
ness she recognised as grief and forced herself into the
morning room, where once more she scanned the classified
advertisements in the newspaper. This time there would be
no decision to stay at Waitapu, no stupid conviction that
she could deal easily with the results of her actions.

First she needed somewhere to stay for the next few
nights while she found a place to live. A friend in a flat
in Grey Lynn wouldn't mind if she dossed down there for
a week or so. Then she had to find a job, otherwise she'd

soon use up the small amount of money she'd have in the bank after she'd repaid Gerard. She looked on the calendar and worked out just how much she owed him.

All right, she told her skipping, racing heart, don't have a panic attack. Calm down. Do this thing in logical steps.

A bed, then a job. That shouldn't be too difficult; she was a good waitress, she could serve behind a fast food counter, or she could work in an old people's home.

Fear kicked her in the stomach. She didn't want to spend the rest of her life working in takeaway shops or waitressing, but what on earth was she to do? A history degree was utterly useless on the job market.

Logic, she reminded herself.

Until she got settled she wouldn't think about the lies Gerard had told, or his reason for telling them.

At least the need to leave Waitapu, the necessity of organising that departure, gave her something to think about and stopped her from giving in to the intense desolation that lay behind the barriers of her will like a howling wasteland.

After a couple of deep breaths she read slowly and carefully through the 'Flatmates Wanted' section. Her heart lifted slightly when she saw that there were still plenty. Having scribbled likely looking numbers down, she turned to the 'Situations Vacant' columns.

Ten minutes later she set the newspaper aside and got up. So close to Christmas very few firms wanted new employees. And what there was wasn't exactly interesting.

'To hell with *interesting*,' she muttered. 'I need to earn a living. Interest can come later.'

She went across to the telephone and began to dial.

CHAPTER NINE

AFTER she'd written down ads and phone numbers to contact in Auckland, Jacinta went back to her room, took out her bank statement and worked out exactly how much money she'd have after she'd repaid Gerard every cent she owed him. It wasn't much, but she'd be able to manage.

She'd have to manage.

Then she wrote a cheque and put it in an envelope on which she wrote his name in big black letters. She'd leave it in her room when she left—Paul would make sure that his cousin got it.

Filled with a desperate need to escape, she told Fran she'd be on the beach, and set off to walk as far and as fast as she could.

Just before dinner, hot and tired, she came back towards the house, watching dotterels bob up and down in avian courtesy, then flow across the sand like silk. These ones were in breeding plumage; no doubt—like the penguins who'd taken over the bach, thereby exposing Jacinta to greater danger than she'd ever envisaged—they had nests nearby.

Warned by some instinct, she looked away from the shiny expanse of sand and saw Paul walk through the barrier of the pohutukawas, his head gleaming like red gold in the sun.

Her heart jumped; she'd never believed that making love could join people in any way other than the purely temporary, but for the rest of her life she'd be living on the memory of the previous night. Oh, she'd get over him, she might even fall in love again, but it would be vastly different from this incandescent emotion.

It was cruel of him to come back while she was still awake, she thought while her treacherous heart rejoiced.

'You're back early,' she said quietly.

'I'm sorry.'

'Why be sorry? This is your home.' The dotterels bowed, and bowed again, then continued their swift gliding across the beach, smooth as skaters. 'Anyway, you won't have to stay in Auckland now if you don't want to. I've found a place to live.'

'Where?'

Surprised at the note of aggression in his voice, she returned coolly, 'In Grey Lynn. It's a mixed flat—two men and three women. It sounds very nice.'

'I see. You haven't met them?'

Her brain spun. Finally she said, 'As it happens, yes. One of the women took the same papers as I did, and during the year we got quite friendly.' Nadia was in Southland for the holidays, but one of her flatmates had rung her and she'd given Jacinta permission to use her bed for as long as she liked.

'When are you going?' he asked flatly.

'I'll catch the bus tomorrow morning.'

He shook his head. 'I'm going down so you might as well come with me.' And before she had time to object he looked past her to the expanse of shining beach, and the small birds going about their age-old ritual. 'I'll have to tell Gerard what happened.'

'Why?'

She could hear his shrug in his voice. 'He should know.'

'So that he can hate you?' she said quietly, knowing she wouldn't make any difference. 'You haven't betrayed him.'

There was silence before he said, 'That's a simplistic attitude. Even if what you say is true, and there is nothing between you, he told me there was because he wanted me to keep away from you. I didn't.'

'So you'll purge a guilt that isn't necessary by ruining your relationship with your cousin.'

He said nothing. Austere, self-sufficient, he looked out to sea, the stark lines of his profile set in iron.

Maddened by her total lack of influence over him, by her helplessness, Jacinta went on, 'I don't understand why he told such lies. Especially as he must know that sooner or later I'd find out. And if he thought that putting me into debt would make me sleep with him—well, he's a throwback to the nineteenth century.' Each word had a bitter, jagged bite to it; she took a moment to compose herself before adding curtly, 'The days are long gone when women could be blackmailed into marriage.'

Paul asked impersonally, 'What are your plans?'

'I've found a job and a place to stay, so neither you nor Gerard need to concern yourselves about me.' She couldn't hold back a savage corollary. 'I've had it up to my teeth with men trying to manipulate me.'

'I'm not trying to manipulate you,' he returned with silky quietness. 'However, I can't help worrying about you.'

'Because I've been so naïve about men?' Infuriatingly, her voice cracked halfway through the sentence. Steadying it, she went on, 'I learn quickly. I'll be all right.'

'And if you're pregnant?' he demanded.

She shook her head. 'It's not likely, is it? We used protection.'

'It has been known to fail,' he said roughly. 'In ten percent of cases, I understand.'

Her shoulders lifted slightly. Staring ahead with eyes that saw nothing, she said, 'I'll face that if it happens.'

'We'll face it,' he said, a hard note warning her that he wouldn't give way.

'All right,' she said quickly.

She lied, of course. If she had his child he would want

to look after her, but she could think of nothing more painful than to be forced to endure constant contact with him. However, she'd deal with that if and when it happened.

The conversation had exhausted her small store of composure; she said, 'I'll go back now. I'll eat in my room.'

Something predatory and coldly reckless splintered in the crystalline eyes. 'Don't hide away because of me,' he said caustically, standing aside to let her past. 'I'm going out tonight.'

How foolish to hope that he'd come back because of her!

He stayed on the beach while she walked away from him into the house, leaving her heart and her innocence behind.

They met at breakfast the next morning. Exhausted after a sleepless night, Jacinta knew that her eyes had dark rings around them, and after a keen glance from Paul wished that she used cosmetics. Good armour, she thought wretchedly. It would have been much better to stick to her guns and leave on the bus; this long-drawn-out farewell was an endurance test, as was eating. Jacinta had to force the food down a throat almost blocked by a knot of grief.

They set off through another brilliant morning, radiant with the promise of heat and humidity. After taping the envelope containing Gerard's cheque to the computer, Jacinta thanked Fran and in spite of Paul's presence asked her to say goodbye to Dean for her.

'Oh,' she said, after Fran had promised to do that, 'I've left a pile of library books beside the bed. Can you take them back?'

'Yes, of course.' Fran looked from Paul's impassive face to Jacinta's, then commanded, 'Take care now, and look after yourself. Make sure you eat your meals on time!'

Jacinta gave her a swift hug and went out to the car. In silence Paul drove towards Auckland; she looked out of the side window until her stomach began to feel queasy, and then she sat staring at the road ahead, noticing nothing.

'What's the address?' he asked halfway across the harbour bridge.

'Drop me in town and I'll get a bus.'

'With two suitcases and those boxes of books? What's the address?'

It would have been a lot easier if he'd let her go, but she hadn't really expected him to. 'Don't you have to be at your office at nine?'

'They can wait.'

It wouldn't be much out of his way because Grey Lynn was one of the inner city suburbs. When the car slid to a stop outside the run-down house Paul asked harshly, 'Is this the best you can do?'

'Students live like this,' she returned with an acid undernote to the words. 'It's quite comfortable inside.'

He got out of the car and opened the boot. Grim-faced, he lifted out her two suitcases and the boxes of books. Jacinta snatched up both suitcases and, panting but determined, carried them through the gate and deposited them at the bottom of the steps before going up the three steps onto the verandah.

She didn't need to knock. The door opened to reveal a tall, thin young man clad only in a villainous overnight shadow and a pair of shorts, who yawned and said, 'Oh, hi, Jacinta.' His gaze went past her to where Paul was bringing the boxes up the path and he straightened up. 'Leave your gear here,' he said. 'I'll bring it inside.'

'Thank you,' Jacinta said again, donning an armour forged of desperation as she swivelled to meet Paul's eyes. 'Goodbye.'

Frowning, he set the boxes down. From the car came the insistent summons of his telephone, and he said brusquely, 'I'll be in contact.'

She watched him go, then turned to the curious gaze of the man in the doorway.

'Thanks,' she said again.

'Think nothing of it, although why you should want to lose a dude like that, heaven knows,' he said, grinning. 'Get a load of that car, will you? He didn't find that in his breakfast cereal.'

From behind her, Jacinta heard the car engine start. Paul acknowledged her wave with a toot, and then the car moved quietly away from the kerb and down the narrow street.

When it was out of sight she gave the man at the door a pale smile and said, 'Nadia said it would be all right if I stayed here until I found board, but with any luck I'll be out of here by tonight.'

'Doesn't matter,' he said cheerfully. 'You can stay as long as you like.'

'And I don't want him to find out where I go.'

'Don't tell me, then,' he said promptly. 'He looks as though he'd know how to get information, that guy—not a good man to cross. But, hey, if I don't know I can't tell him, can I?'

'And don't tell him where Nadia is, either.' It was unlikely, but if Paul really wanted to find out where she was he'd turn on the charm and Nadia, notoriously susceptible, would tell him everything.

He shrugged. 'Don't know that, either. Yesterday when I rang for you she was talking about going to Sydney to work.'

He helped her take the cases and boxes inside and stack them in the hallway. She'd done her best to cover her tracks, because it was just Paul's sense of responsibility that would make him want her address.

And she had no intention of telling Carl, he of the shorts and unshaven chin, where she was going. She didn't know herself yet.

'Can I use your phone? And have you got a bus timetable?' she asked.

*   *   *

At four-thirty that afternoon she was unpacking in a room on the other side of town. Of the same vintage as Nadia's, the house was charming and sunny, surrounded by a somewhat overgrown cottage garden in which the white trumpet flowers of a datura hung dramatically against a hedge, their heavy scent almost banishing the persistent petrol fumes.

A cheerful woman about her own age owned the place. 'There's another woman living here—it's a flat situation, although you're both helping me pay the mortgage,' she'd said, when they'd met in her lunch hour. 'Shall we say a month to see if we all get on well?'

'Sounds fine to me,' Jacinta had agreed.

She sat down on the single bed. It would help, she thought wearily, if she could cry, but although she was locked into an aching, desolate grief, no tears came.

Just as well, because the next day she had to find a job.

It took her a week, but by the end of it she was behind the counter in a bookshop, a small, busy affair in the next suburb which sold mostly paperbacks. Although she was on a month's trial, at least it removed her immediate financial worry. At the end of the first day she rested her aching feet and legs in her room and made a list of goals.

She would work two hours a day on the manuscript, because now that was the only promise she could keep to her mother. Writing by hand was going to be slow, but she'd get there.

She would not think of Paul more than five times a day.

This one she couldn't keep, but she became adept at turning her mind away from him.

She would think seriously about her future—a future empty of Paul.

That became less frightening when she realised that she enjoyed working in the bookshop, and that she had a talent for helping people find what they wanted to read. Although the money wasn't too good she managed to survive on it, and when, just before Christmas, the owner of the store asked her if she'd like to work there permanently she was delighted.

So now she had two goals. She'd finish the manuscript and one day she'd own her own bookshop.

Three goals. One day she'd say the word 'Paul' and feel no more than a mildly regretful reminiscence.

It surprised her that her grief was so different from that she'd endured after her mother's death, which had been tempered by relief that Cynthia no longer suffered. This was bone-deep and bitter, with the added edge of physical loss. During the hot nights she'd dream of Paul, then wake, eager and expectant, her body singing with anticipation and memories.

That was bad, but what was worse was the small things she remembered—the way his mouth had quirked when she'd said something he considered funny, the gilt of his hair beneath the sun, the tanned strength of his hands, his elusive male scent, faint yet so powerful that it still clung to the recesses of her brain.

And the way he walked, lithe, unconsciously predatory, with the smooth power of perfect health and strong, masculine grace.

This must have been how her mother felt. But Jacinta was not to have a permanent reminder of the man she loved; there would be no baby. It was a profound relief, yet the arrival of her period added another layer to the burden of her days.

Striving to deal with the memories, she got on with her life. As the summer days heated and the humidity intensified she discovered that she had passed all of her examinations, so was now able to put the letters BA after her name. With the knowledge came a sense of closure, of finality.

Christmas was every bit as agonising as she'd imagined it would be. Both of her flatmates invited her to spend the day itself with them and their families, but for some reason—masochism, she decided—she wanted to be alone. So she stayed in the house and wrote.

Afterwards she thought, Nothing is ever going to be as bad as that again. Next year will be better.

One weekend at the beginning of a hot and sticky January she opened the door to an insistent ring. Oddly enough she wasn't surprised when her eyes met hard, bright blue ones. Deep inside she'd known that Paul would find her.

She was alone, so she said, 'Come on in,' and fell back as he came through the door like a force of nature, silently, his bearing proclaiming an implacable purposefulness that should have intimidated her.

Instead she felt rejuvenated.

'How are you?' she asked, leading him into the sitting room.

'Do you care?'

Taking a deep breath, she steadied her voice and lifted her chin. 'Of course I care.'

'So much so that you deliberately lied to me. And don't tell me you didn't say a word—you didn't have to. Losing me was a clever piece of work.'

The cold condemnation in his tone cut her composure to shreds, but she managed to say, 'Sit down. How did you find me?'

'I put a private detective onto you,' he told her, watching her as though even then he expected her to try and run. 'He targeted libraries. But you didn't join any library until three days ago.'

Because she'd been reading her way through the stock in the shop. The owner felt it was important she know what her customers were buying.

'It seems an awful lot of trouble,' she said carefully.

'I went to see Gerard,' he astounded her by saying, his hooded gaze fixed onto her face.

'Why? No, don't tell me. I don't want to hear anything about it.'

'Tough,' he said. 'Sit down.'

She defied him a moment with jutted chin, then sank into a chair. His eyes were polished brighter than lapis lazuli—completely opaque—and she could see he wasn't going until she'd heard him out.

Before he could say anything she said, 'I'm not in love with him. I've never been in love with him; it's utterly incredible that he claimed to be in love with me.' Her voice was level and emotionless; her heart was shattering.

'Oh, he wanted you,' Paul said between his teeth.

'I feel now as though he was stalking me.'

'I don't blame you.' He frowned, and she knew that the interview with Gerard hadn't been easy for him, or pleasant.

After a moment he said evenly, 'He was afraid to try his luck.'

'I don't understand,' she said, fighting the feeling of helplessness that still assailed her when she thought of Gerard's stealthy pursuit. 'Why didn't he come out into the open?'

'It's no excuse, but he lacks confidence. His mother is one of those people who are experts at snide put-downs. His father didn't even bother to be snide. He wanted a big, strong, athletic son who'd make the All Blacks and follow him into the family business. Instead Gerard became an academic. I suspect he found the idea of actually opening himself up to rejection terrifying.'

'Even so,' Jacinta said stonily, 'he must have known that what he was doing was—'

'Sinister? He doesn't see it that way. He wanted to help you but he knew you'd never take money from him, so he did what he could for you.' He paused, then said, 'He said you were desperate to get away from the flat you were living in.'

'I—' Jacinta drew in a deep breath. 'Yes,' she said, looking down at her hands. 'Yes, I was. But I had organised a place to go to—the house in Grey Lynn where you dropped me off. I knew I'd be able to doss down with Nadia for as long as it took me to find somewhere else to stay. Unfortunately she was away on a field trip, and I had to wait a week before she came back.'

'Did he—the man you were living with—beat you?' He spoke with a chilling lack of emotion that pulled the hairs on the back of her neck upright.

'No! Not so long ago I read a book about psychological abusers, and Mark fits all the signs. I met him just after my mother died, when I was moving out of the house we rented; he was staying with the family who owned it. He was Mrs Atkinson's nephew; anyway, I suppose I trusted him because they could vouch for him. He was very kind and sympathetic, and I was—'

'Vulnerable.'

She closed her eyes for a second. 'Oh, yes, very vulnerable,' she admitted. 'And swept away. He organised the flat for me—until I moved in I didn't know that he lived there too. I wasn't able to even conceive of any sort of romantic relationship then. I was just too tired.'

'So you weren't lovers?' He spoke austerely.

'No.' She frowned, trying to recall those miserable months. 'I thought he was wonderful because he could make me laugh,' she said at length. 'But when I moved in he changed. At first I didn't see it; he did everything for me—ran errands, made it so that I had no responsibilities, took me to the campus and picked me up—cosseted me in every way. I couldn't work out why, instead of wallowing in it after all those years when I'd had to be strong, I was so—so uneasy. And he manipulated me by putting on a sad face if I did anything he didn't want so that I felt I was hurting him. He didn't exactly sulk—although that's what it was, really. It all came to a head when I went to a party with Nadia—'

She stopped and he said curtly, 'Go on.'

'Mark didn't want me to go, and when I did he made me feel that I'd done something terrible—wounded him to the quick. After that I noticed that he resented anything I did that he hadn't organised. And then I found out that he'd been reading my mail and monitoring my phone calls, deciding who should talk to me and who shouldn't. That was when I realised I had to get out.'

'And Gerard offered you board.' He spoke without expression.

'I wasn't going to jump from the frying pan into the fire, so I turned him down. Then he mentioned the flat.' Jacinta sent him a swift glance, then let her gaze fall. 'The night before Gerard found me asleep in the library I'd told Mark I was leaving. He horrified me and astounded me by insisting that I couldn't go, that he was in love with me and he was nothing without me. I—I didn't know what to say. He kept me up all night pleading with me. That was why I was exhausted. But I didn't tell Gerard anything about Mark,' she finished. 'I was ashamed that I'd let myself get into such a situation.'

'He knew, nevertheless.'

'Apparently.' Her hands lay tense in her lap, still dusted with gold by Waitapu sun. She said slowly, 'But nothing gave Gerard the right to think that he had—bought me. Why did he tell you we were engaged?'

A thin wash of colour appeared over Paul's angular cheekbones. 'He's always been envious of me. In spite of my break-up with Aura he pretends to believe that I have no difficulty with women,' he said unsparingly.

Jacinta narrowed her eyes. 'Possibly,' she said dulcetly, 'because you don't.'

'That's ridiculous, and you, of all women, should know it. Gerard understands how important loyalty is to me, so he was reasonably sure I wouldn't try to seduce the woman he was engaged to. And whether he believed it or not—I think he did—he told me you were looking for security. I assumed you were using him, which is why I was so rude to you when you arrived.'

She said bleakly, 'You were distant, but not rude.'

'I wanted you the minute I saw you in Fiji,' he said with a savage smile. 'And when I danced with you I thought you weren't indifferent to me. But I could see that the last thing you needed was any emotional involvement—you were wrapped up with your mother. I wanted to help you both, but you and Cynthia were so linked that in some odd way I felt I'd be intruding. However, I had your address. I rang about six weeks after you'd come back, and the wife of the man who owned the house you rented told me that your mother had died and you'd moved into a flat with a man in Auckland.'

Astonished, Jacinta stared at him. His mouth shaped a cynical smile. 'So I wrote you off as just another woman who preferred another man. And then you turned up as Gerard's fiancée. I could have broken his neck when he told me your name.'

Jacinta said shakily, 'I don't believe this.'

'Why? You must know the effect you have on men.'

Stunned, she shook her head, and he said, 'When I reminded you that Dean was engaged, I wasn't thinking of Brenda. It was far more primitive than that. I was eaten up with jealousy. I had no reason to disbelieve Gerard, and to me it seemed that you were flirting with Dean, with Harry Moore, even with Laurence.'

She stared at him. 'I was being friendly,' she retorted scathingly.

A mocking smile—humourless, hard—twisted his mouth. 'And I wasn't being reasonable,' he said, his amusement directed at himself. 'I thought—Damn it, she flirts with everyone else, why not with me? You let Dean touch you—you laughed when he tickled your foot—but every time I laid a finger on you you leapt away as though I was poison.'

In a quiet, uneven voice Jacinta said, 'I was afraid. Of myself. Of the way I felt.'

'So,' he said grimly, 'was I. I realised very early after you came to Waitapu that I was in too deep; the only honourable thing to do was to pull away, and I tried. I travelled—God, I left the country every chance I could—but I couldn't stay away from Waitapu. And that first physical attraction was supported and strengthened when I found that you were intelligent and funny and easy to talk to, that I liked just being with you, that I longed for the end of the day when I could come home and talk to you.'

Jacinta's hands tightened into knots in her lap. His voice was steady, almost thoughtful, but although she understood the words and sentences, she couldn't believe them.

'And then,' he said, rawness roughening his tone, 'I made love to you, and it was the most wonderful thing that has ever happened to me. Were you a virgin, Jacinta?'

Her knuckles ached as her grip tightened. 'Yes,' she said almost inaudibly.

He made a smothered sound and she looked up, to see the strong features compressed in what looked suspiciously like pain. 'I didn't know,' he said, mastering his expression so swiftly she thought she must be mistaken. 'Afterwards I realised that you were so surprised—so—so innocent—and I wondered. But you ran away and I couldn't find you. Do you know what you did to me?'

She refused to meet his eyes. 'I had to go.'

'Because I drove you away? Because I didn't believe you when you told me Gerard had lied?'

'Partly.' Her throat was dry and parched, as though she'd been without water for days.

Paul walked across to the window and looked out at the roses on the edge of the terrace. The sun streamed in, gilding his profile. Blinking as she stole a swift glance, Jacinta's heart tightened within her chest. He looked tired, she thought anxiously, that dynamic power dimmed.

'When I turned up at Gerard's temporary lodgings in Massachusetts the week after you left—and the gods must be laughing at this—he was not particularly glad to see me. I'd arrived at an awkward time.'

Jacinta shivered.

'He was in bed with a woman,' Paul finished, swinging to look at her, sitting there with the merciless light of the sun illuminating her every feature.

She said in a bewildered voice, 'Who?'

'An American. When she'd gone he admitted—very reluctantly—that he'd lied when he'd claimed to be engaged to you. He thought he was in love with you, and he was certain that if I thought so too I'd keep well away from you. He was wrong on both counts. Apparently he's really fallen in love this time, and he wants to marry her.'

Explosively, Jacinta said, 'I'll *kill* him—does he have any idea of what he did?'

Just caused weeks of misery and pain!

Grimly, Paul said, 'If he didn't before, he does now, believe me. I was not tactful.' He came and sat down beside her, taking her cold hands in his warm clasp. 'Jacinta,' he said, his voice deep and caressing, his eyes bluer than the sky at midday, 'come back to Waitapu with me. I've missed you so much that I can't even eat without remembering you. You took all the colour from my life when you fled. Bring it back.'

He meant it, she could tell, and he was totally confident that she would come.

'I can't,' she said quietly.

His head came up. For a terrifying moment she saw the Viking in his eyes, determined, possessive, ruthless. With lips that barely moved, in a voice so silkily soft she had to strain to hear it, he asked, 'Why?'

'I can't live with you when you're still in love with another woman.'

Sheer male satisfaction gleamed in his eyes. 'So you do love me,' he said, his smile tight and feral.

Wrenching her hands free, she folded them again in her lap and said in a dead voice, 'Yes, I love you. I wouldn't have slept with you if I hadn't loved you. But it's no use. You might not think you're still in love with Aura, but since she left you no woman's ever got close to you.'

'You have,' he said curtly, his eyes watchful, almost calculating.

Colour fired her skin. Almost she wavered, but a gritty, uncompromising stubbornness urged her on. 'Am I the first woman you've made love to since she left you?'

His brows drew together. 'No. I am not, however, still in love with Aura.'

She wanted to believe him so much that the wanting ate into her heart. Her determination almost wavered, almost let her take the easy path. But she couldn't rid herself of the memory of his face when he'd seen the woman he'd once been engaged to on that scrap of video film.

Whatever emotions he still felt for Aura had not been resolved. Jacinta had lived, she thought with sudden blinding clarity, a second-hand life. Instead of striking out on her own she'd fulfilled her mother's thwarted ambitions, and although she didn't regret that, she was not going to take second-best for love. She wanted Paul intensely, but she wanted all of him, not the hand-me-down love he offered.

If she surrendered to her own driving needs without that commitment from him, her love would eventually degenerate into an angry passion diluted by resentful yearning.

The stark moment of insight gave her the strength to continue. 'Do you ever talk to her when you see her at parties and social occasions?'

'No.'

She thought that was going to be his sole answer, but he got up and walked across the room, his shoulders set, his spine straight as a steel rod. At the window he swung around and looked at her. His voice was cool, detached, glacial. 'I haven't spoken to either of them since the day Aura told me she wasn't marrying me.'

Jacinta waited. He remained silent, so eventually she said huskily, 'Her husband was your best friend, yet you haven't said a word to him for five years. Even if you aren't in love with her—and I think you are—she still controls your life.'

'What the hell do you mean by that?' he asked, each word falling distinctly into the still air.

She wouldn't retreat. 'Would you be happy if she walked into this room right now?'

As the rigidity of his expression gave her the answer a hope—so fragile she hadn't been aware of its existence—died.

To have heaven offered to her and be forced to turn it down...

Stiffly he said, 'No.'

At least he didn't try to explain or excuse his response. 'Paul, it won't work.'

Fury glittered, dangerous as lightning, in the blue of his eyes. 'What do you want?' he demanded. 'I love you, but I'm not going to—'

She had to interrupt before he broke her heart. 'It won't work,' she repeated, unable to think of anything else to say. 'I'm sorry.'

He didn't beg, but then she didn't expect him to. 'In that case,' he said with dangerous calmness, 'there's nothing I can do.'

Jacinta sat still, her urgent heart shouting, Give in, give in.

With a cold-blooded calculation, Paul said, 'I assume you're not pregnant.'

'I'm not.'

'Good. And you don't need to run away from me; I won't be bothering you again.'

Surprisingly enough, she coped.

Work helped. She lost more weight, but she forced herself to make friends, to go out, to ignore the ravening physical hunger that tore at her, and the even more insidious need to hold Paul close, to hear his voice, to see him.

But she never managed to banish him entirely from her

mind, and several times she almost gave up and went back to Waitapu to see if he still wanted her. Each time an instinct stronger than need warned her that she wasn't able to compromise so drastically. For her, it seemed, it had to be all or nothing.

Summer dragged wearily on; she still enjoyed the shop, liked the two women she shared the house with, stoically endured the slow process of making some sort of life for herself. As autumn swept in, with mellow days and cooler nights and a blessed reduction of humidity, she finished her manuscript and began to doggedly edit and rewrite.

Once she saw an article in the newspaper raving over the introduction of a new wine; it was not normally something that would have interested her, but the name 'Aura' sprang out and snared her attention. Angry with herself for wilfully adding to her pain, she read about the superb red which was already a classic, grown some forty miles north of Auckland. It had been released with an enormous amount of fanfare—orchestrated by the vintner's wife, Aura Jansen. The wine writer was obviously in love with the woman as well as the wine.

'Join the gang,' Jacinta said viciously.

There was a photograph. Even in the newspaper shot the woman's beauty shone forth, warm and ripe and—loved, Jacinta thought as her gaze went from Aura Jansen to the man beside her.

She sucked in a deep breath. This fiercely dominating man had been Paul's best friend. Not handsome, no, far from it, yet Flint Jansen's starkly hewn buccaneer's face drew the eye.

As she threw the newspaper out she thought that it said a lot about Paul's personality. He looked a golden man, one of fortune's darlings, yet beneath that handsome exterior was a wild streak, buttressed by force of personality and a formidable will that could break bones.

And hearts, she thought.

Oh, it would be so easy to take what he offered.

And her will was every bit as strong as his, because she couldn't do it, couldn't surrender herself and her life to a man who valued her only as second-best.

A couple of days later a sudden foretaste of winter whipped a cold southerly wind through the city, accompanied by swift showers that brought with them the acrid scent of long-dry roads and pavements. As it was Jacinta's turn to buy the groceries, she was carrying two large bags from the bus when she tripped in a puddle and skidded onto her knee, dropping one bag.

Muttering maledictions, she dragged herself up and stumbled on her way. With the malice of fate the plastic bag, weakened by its collision with the wet pavement, waited until she was halfway up the front steps before it burst.

Furious, she raced up and dumped what she'd been able to save by the door, then set off to pick up the cauliflower that had bounced all the way down. It didn't surprise her in the least when she slipped on the last step and landed in a puddle put there expressly for that purpose.

The cauliflower was there before her, lying in the muddy water with its florets buried. She'd probably have to disinfect it before it was fit to eat.

'Oh, hell!' Jacinta spluttered.

Two hard hands grabbed her shoulders and with a swift, smooth movement hauled her upright. Confounded, she stared into eyes the clear, fierce blue of a summer sky.

And realised just how much she'd been lying to herself since she'd last seen him. To her horror and astonishment, she began to cry.

'You've hurt yourself,' Paul said harshly. 'Where? Your ankle? Your knee? Jacinta, stop that and tell me where it hurts!'

'I'm not hurt,' she sobbed. 'Not physically, damn you! How dare you come here and—'

'We have to talk. Do you want me to carry you up the steps?'

'No!' She pushed him away.

Instantly she felt bereft, her addiction fed and intensified by the few moments spent hugged against his hard body. She turned, but remembered the cauliflower and stooped to retrieve it. With jangling nerves and an odd emptiness in her stomach, she led the way into the house, walking straight past the rest of the groceries.

Paul scooped them up, and followed her down the chilly hall and into the kitchen. As soon as he'd dumped the bags onto the bench he turned and surveyed her.

'Good,' he said, 'I'm not the only one who's suffered. Will you come back with me to Waitapu?'

Tears ached in her throat and behind her eyes. Swallowing, she shook her head.

His smile was sharp and brutal as a bayonet. 'Yet you love me.'

It was useless trying to deny it. She nodded and went to put the cauliflower, still dripping with water from the puddle and probably inedible, into the sink.

'I went to see Aura and Flint,' Paul said casually.

The vegetable fell from her nerveless fingers and thudded onto stainless steel. Jacinta stared at it without seeing it, her whole attention on the man who stood behind her. 'Why?' she asked in a thin voice.

'Because I decided you could be right.'

God, she was an idiot. 'I know I am,' she muttered.

'In one thing only,' he amended swiftly. 'I proved that I'm certainly no longer in love with Aura, but you were right in that I needed to see her.'

Hope blew faintly on Jacinta's dreams, warming the embers. Jumpy, her pulses racing, she turned and began to pick up the groceries from the faded bench that had been someone's idea of high kitchen fashion in the seventies and stack them into the pantry.

'Leave those alone, for heaven's sake.'

A voice from the door enquired, 'Jacinta, is everything all right?'

'Yes, no problems,' Jacinta said swiftly.

'Oh. OK.' The owner of the house retreated down the hall.

Paul said curtly, 'I have to see you alone. Come for a drive with me.'

She couldn't think, could barely breathe—so completely focused on the man behind her that she sensed his movements and stiffened even before his hand fastened onto her arm and he swung her to face him.

'You look like a ghost,' he said, his voice deepening into concern.

Ignoring her resistance, he pulled her into his arms, surrounding her with warmth and strength and the wonderful male scent of him.

'Darling,' he muttered, a note she'd never heard before in his voice. 'What have I done to you? How can I convince you that I love you more than I ever loved Aura, who has turned out to be a very nice woman—'

It was that last comment that fanned the embers of hope into a small flame. Startled, she lifted her face and asked incredulously, 'A nice woman?'

His eyes were blue and fierce, lit by a tiny glint of humour. 'Yes,' he said seriously, his mouth ironic. 'A very nice woman. Oh, marriage and happiness has made her even more beautiful, but that sultry glamour that ensnared me before no longer has any power over me. I looked at her, and although I enjoyed her beauty I felt nothing but interest and a wry sort of friendship. You were right. I'd managed to convince myself that I'd buried my heart along with our engagement. Oh, not consciously, and in a way I'm glad it happened—'

'Why?' she repeated, back on the roller-coaster again.

'Because I might have given in earlier to my desire for a settled family life and children, and got married.'

Her heart lurched. He was looking at her with naked intensity, the good humour and confidence stripped from him to reveal the man beneath, a man consumed by his emotions.

At that moment she believed. 'Then I'm glad too,' she whispered, losing herself in the vivid clarity of his gaze. He bent his head, but from down the hallway came the sound of more footsteps. Paul said something curt and crisp beneath his breath and let Jacinta go.

'Let's go,' he said grimly. 'We can't talk here.'

Jacinta nodded, and went with him. The showers had stopped coming, and to the west the sky was a clear, sparkling blue beneath an arch of cloud. Jacinta looked at the neighbour's dahlias, glowing in colours so hot they almost hurt the eyes, set bravely against the dark hedge.

Once in the car Paul said, 'We can go back to my flat.'

For some reason she didn't want to. She said, 'No, let's go up One Tree Hill.'

He gave her an ironic glance, but drove there, winding up the side of the small extinct volcano until they reached the car park at the summit. Neither said anything on the way, nor did they speak until Paul had switched off the ignition and they'd both gazed for a short time at the panorama below, city and seascape, small volcanic domes and parks. Up on the grassy hill, they were separated from the everyday bustle and hurry.

Paul said, 'I began to fall in love with you the first time I saw you at Waitapu.'

'You despised me,' she said indignantly.

'Not as much as I despised myself for wanting the woman who was using Gerard.'

She flinched, and he said swiftly, 'I couldn't keep on believing that.'

'But you accused me of it after we'd spent the night together.'

Paul turned his head to look at her. She glowered back. His handsome face was taut, his eyes very bright and piercing as they held hers.

'I was running away,' he said, choosing his words carefully, 'behaving like a coward. By then I couldn't believe Gerard, but I knew that whatever I felt for you wasn't something I could control. Right from the start I was in a fight I couldn't win; half of me was trying to convince myself that you were just looking for security, the other, clearer-eyed, half insisted that the honesty I saw in your eyes was the truth. But that I was falling in love—so much that I no longer cared whether you were engaged to him— no, I wouldn't face that.'

Jacinta thought she understood. 'And that's why you fought it, because you hated losing control. I suppose that's how you felt with Aura.'

He shook his head. 'No, that's what frightened me,' he admitted. 'I thought I loved her, yet there was simply no comparison. I couldn't analyse the emotions you caused— they were too bloody fresh and painful and overwhelming, and they scared the hell out of me.'

She blinked. 'I kept telling myself that attraction wasn't the same as falling in love,' she confessed shakily. 'I didn't believe in love at first sight, therefore it had to be sex.'

'Idiots, both of us. I knew I had no right to make love to you; I'd done to Gerard exactly what Aura did to me.' He smiled without humour, self-condemning. 'My cowardice and refusal to accept that I'd actually fallen in love with you persuaded me to drive you away. But I had no intention of losing sight of you.'

She looked out across the harbour. A small plane newly escaped from the pull of gravity soared into the east and headed away. 'I know,' she said.

'I learned,' he said in a clipped, tight voice, 'that the small amount of honour I'd salvaged was no recompense for the agony of not knowing where you were, of sleeping each night in an empty bed that seemed scented by your body. So I set my bloodhound on your track, and went to see Gerard. And when I found you again, you turned me down.'

'I love you too much to be second-best,' she said quietly. 'But, oh, it was the most enormous temptation, and I don't know how long I'd have held out.'

'Good,' he said with a satisfaction that swung perilously close to arrogance. 'And you were right, of course. I needed to see Aura again.'

Jacinta understood. She said, 'And now you're sure.'

'Not about you. I need to know,' he said, his voice thickened and uneven, 'whether you'll marry me.' His smile twisted. 'My life isn't worth much without you. I go through the motions but I don't seem to be actually alive. When you left me, Jacinta, you took the sun with you.'

And then the smile vanished, to be replaced by a hard line. 'Oh, what the hell?' he said unsteadily. 'I can't even fool myself any longer. I need you so intensely, so passionately, that I have no defences. That's what infuriated me and scared me when I saw you in Fiji. I'd been burnt once—I had no intention of letting myself fall in thraldom to another *belle dame sans merci*.'

'Is that what Aura is? A beautiful, merciless woman?'

'No,' he said on a harsh breath. 'And neither are you. It was a shoddy little piece of self-deception on my part. Jacinta—'

With troubled eyes she interrupted. 'What about the woman who was in Fiji with you?'

'She's a good friend who needed time off to get over a situation she'd found herself in. We weren't lovers.'

Jacinta believed him, but she had to probe further. 'Gerard pointed out a woman in Ponsonby one day—'

'We broke up after I came back from that trip,' he said, his gaze holding hers. 'We'd been lovers for over a year, but I was never in love with her, nor she with me. After Fiji I knew it had come to an end. I hated leaving you there—I wanted to snatch you up and somehow make everything right for you, but I couldn't.'

'Nobody could,' she said soberly. 'We had to get through it together, Mum and I. In the end she died a lot sooner than we thought she would.'

'I didn't see the death notice. I was going to write.'

'I only put it in the local paper.'

He gave a short, unamused laugh. 'And then you turned up as Gerard's fiancée, and from that first night at Waitapu I knew just how much trouble I was in. You said you'd never tasted champagne, and I wanted to be the one who introduced you to all the things you'd never known.'

Jacinta said, 'You hid it very well!'

His smile was sardonic and self-derisory. 'Did I? I thought I was very easy to read. What really got me worried was that for days at a time it was perilously easy to forget all about Gerard.'

'But sometimes you remembered,' she said softly, recalling the times when he'd 'gone away', changing from the Paul she'd been falling in love with to a distant, grimmer man.

'Then I'd look at you and think, She's nothing like Aura.' His mouth hardened into a straight line. 'In fact, that's one of the reasons I first fell in love with you. You are her exact opposite.'

It hurt, but she couldn't let him see that. As the beautiful face of the woman he'd loved and lost flashed into her mind she said, 'Very much so.'

He laughed, a cynical sound with no humour. 'Don't put yourself down, Jacinta. On the night of the party I realised that you had the same passionate allure as Aura, and I thought, I've done it again.'

'I'm not—'

'You looked just like that picture Laurence Perry said you reminded him of—Leighton's *Flaming June*. When I saw the print I understood exactly what he saw—a luscious, totally, splendidly over-the-top woman reeking with lazy, seductive sensuousness. I wanted to drag you off to bed away from everyone else—and I despised myself for wanting you so much.'

'Paul, I know those colours look good on me, but—'

'Every man at that party was slavering at the jaws,' he

said. Blue fire heated his eyes. 'Although I'm possessive I can control it, but that night I was eaten up with jealousy and desire and disgusted anger with myself.'

'So that's why you were so cold.'

'Yes.'

'Did you make love to Meriam Anderson?' she demanded fiercely.

He lifted his head. 'No. I didn't want to, and even if I had, I don't use women to appease a meaningless hunger.'

Jacinta was ashamed, but she said, 'She gave the impression that you were together, and you did nothing to change it.'

'I was running scared. I wanted you out of my life and as far away from me as possible, but I knew I couldn't throw you out because I'd promised bloody Gerard.' His voice hardened. 'I didn't know what to do, so I used Meriam in that way.'

She laughed softly. 'I thought you were so rational, so level-headed.'

'I used to think so too, but cowardice makes fools of us all. I didn't want to make love to you—I knew it would only complicate things—but when you touched me that night nothing could have stopped me. I'd starved for you, become obsessed with you, and at that moment I'd have killed to get you into my bed.'

Chills ran down her spine, pulled her skin taut. 'I know,' she said slowly. 'I knew it was dangerous, but—I was like you.'

'Then I drove you away.' His fingers drummed a few seconds on the steering wheel, fell still. In silence they watched a huge plane swoop low over the city before landing at the airport some miles away.

Without looking at her, Paul said roughly, 'And when I found you again I thought that everything would be all right, that you'd fall into my arms and we'd be happy together. But you refused to have anything to do with me, and I walked out in a monumental temper. I had to go

overseas for ten days, and when I came back I hoped you'd
be at Waitapu, waiting for me. It took me quite a while to
realise that you weren't going to give in. So I wangled an
invitation to the launching of Flint and Aura's new wine.'

'Were they pleased to see you?' she asked.

'I think so.'

He leaned over and took her hands in his big, warm
clasp, pulling them up to lie over his heart. 'We might
become friends again,' he said with a calm detachment that
was belied by the thundering pulse beneath her palm. 'And
if we do I'll be glad, because I've missed them both. But
you—I more than miss you. I ache for you at night and I
get up and walk the beach, remembering the night we
made love, and the way you tasted, sweet and tempting
and mysterious, and the ache turns into a hard, hot hunger
that drives me insane.'

'Oh, yes,' she said, and was drawn into the warm security of his arms. 'Like losing half of myself, like dying
slowly by inches, like walking alone through a world of
grey emptiness…'

'Never again,' he said, and the words were a vow.
'Never again, my heart, my glorious, summer girl, I
swear.'

CHAPTER TEN

JACINTA MCALPINE slid into the slip dress of gold satin and surveyed herself in the mirror. Her hair, caught up into a demure knot at the back of her head, glowed in the light of the lamp.

She looked good, she thought, allowing herself a slightly immodest satisfaction. A year ago she'd never have worn a dress like this. It revealed an awful lot of skin.

But then a year ago she'd only been married for six months and she'd still found it difficult to see herself through Paul's eyes. Now she knew she looked good in the vivid, tawny sunset hues that made the most of her hair and eyes and colouring. And the happiness of being loved had given her grace at last; it was quite some time since the last time she'd tripped.

She grinned wickedly at the framed print tucked behind the door. *Flaming June*, indeed!

'Ready, darling?' Paul came through from the bedroom, stopping just inside the door. 'You look like high summer,' he said, eyes kindling.

'We both look very glamorous,' she told him, adjusting his black bow tie with a languorous finger. 'Evening clothes do something electric to your hair and eyes,' she said softly, tracing very lightly the contours of his mouth. 'And yes, I'm ready.'

He laughed deeply, catching her hand and kissing the palm before his other hand emerged from behind his back, a ribbon of fire running through his fingers. 'Not quite ready, not yet. Turn around,' he said.

The stones were gorgeous, in a modern setting of gold that enhanced their magnificent colour. Paul put the necklace around her throat and did up the clasp.

'Paul, you spoil me. They're so beautiful—thank you. What are they?' Jacinta leaned back into the warm solidity of him as she surveyed their images in the mirror. Strong and lithe and safe, she thought dreamily; he was the rock-solid base for her life, because the dynamic power and intensity, the spice of danger, were leashed firmly by his mastery of himself and his emotions.

'Padparadscha sapphires,' he said, his hands coming to rest on her shoulders. 'It's a Singhalese word meaning lotus blossom. Did you know that "jacinth" was the word used for the colour orange until oranges came on the scene in the Middle Ages?'

'No,' she said, shivering as he slid his hands beneath her breasts. They tingled, subtly expanding, and through the gold silk she saw the nipples bud.

'That's what your name means. It's the Spanish form of the Greek word for hyacinth.'

'Hyacinth?' She turned her head. 'Really? I've never seen an orange hyacinth. I have seen hyacinths the colour of your eyes, though.'

'Perhaps there used to be orange hyacinths in ancient Greece,' he murmured, his serene expression belying the glitter of his eyes. 'The stones suit you—they look like flames around that elegant throat.'

Because she needed to think, she pulled his hands down to her waist and held them still. 'I got a phone call from America today.'

'America?' He'd bent to kiss the pale skin of her shoulder, but now his head came up.

'Yes.' She met his eyes in the mirror, hers shimmering with gold. 'It was the editor I sent the manuscript to. Paul, they want to publish it!'

'I knew it,' he said triumphantly. 'I knew you'd get there one day. When?'

'Some months after the baby's born, I imagine,' she said sweetly.

He went very still. 'I didn't know we were pregnant,' he said eventually in a neutral voice.

'Neither did I until today. Do you mind?'

His arms tightened around her. In a voice she'd never heard him use before, he said, 'When I look at you I see everything there is—in this world and the next—for me to love. Even delighted doesn't exactly describe how I feel. Thrilled—ecstatic—no, exalted probably describes it best.'

He turned her and kissed her, gently and then with increasing ardour, so that she gasped and yielded, some dim part of her brain remembering to be grateful that she hadn't yet put on lipstick.

And then she didn't think for a long time. Eighteen months of marriage had proved entirely wrong the old adage that familiarity bred contempt. Jacinta still shivered with anticipation whenever she saw her husband, and their lovemaking was sweet and fiercely tender and heated, a wild, rapturous joining of bodies and souls.

'How do you feel?' he asked later, when she was stroking colour onto her slightly tender lips.

'Great. Shall we tell anyone or keep it a secret?'

He laughed. 'Darling, we'll do whatever you want to, although isn't there some female Mafia that knows exactly when a woman is pregnant?'

She put the lipstick down and gave him a saucy grin. 'Let's see if Aura realises.'

He dropped a kiss on her head. 'I love you so much,' he said, his voice steady and sure and vibrant. 'You've gathered all the sunlight in the world into yourself and surrounded me with it.'

Jacinta sighed and whispered, 'If Aura and Flint weren't celebrating their gold medal wine I'd suggest we stay home. But one day soon we'll want their help to celebrate a book, so we'd better go. Afterwards…'

Hand in hand, they went out and into their future.

Looking For More Romance?

Visit Romance.net

Check in daily for these and other exciting features:

Hot off the press

View all current titles, and purchase them on-line.

What do the stars have in store for you?

Horoscope

Hot deals

Exclusive offers available only at Romance.net

Plus, don't miss our interactive quizzes, contests and bonus gifts.

PWEB

Coming Next Month

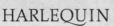 HARLEQUIN PRESENTS®

THE BEST HAS JUST GOTTEN BETTER!

#2013 CONTRACT BABY Lynne Graham
(The Husband Hunters)
Becoming a surrogate mother was Polly's only option when her mother needed a life-saving operation. But the baby's father was businessman Raul Zaforteza, and he would do anything to keep his unborn child—even marry Polly....

#2014 THE MARRIAGE SURRENDER Michelle Reid
(Presents Passion)
When Joanna had no choice but to turn to her estranged husband, Sandro, for help, he agreed, but on one condition: that she return to his bed—as his wife. But what would happen when he discovered her secret?

#2015 THE BRIDE WORE SCARLET Diana Hamilton
When Daniel Faber met his stepbrother's mistress, Annie Kincaid, he decided the only way he could keep her away from his stepbrother was to kidnap her! But the plan had a fatal flaw—Daniel had realized he wanted Annie for himself!

#2016 DANTE'S TWINS Catherine Spencer
(Expecting!)
it wasn't just jealous colleagues who believed Leila was marrying for money; so did her boss, and fiancé Dante Rossi! How could Leila marry him without convincing him she was more than just the mother of his twins?

#2017 ONE WEDDING REQUIRED! Sharon Kendrick
(Wanted: One Wedding Dress)
Amber was delighted to be preparing to marry her boss, hunky Finn Fitzgerald. But after she gave an ill-advised interview to an unscrupulous journalist, it seemed there wasn't going to be a wedding at all....

#2018 MISSION TO SEDUCE Sally Wentworth
Allie was certain she didn't need bodyguard Drake Marsden for her assignment in Russia. But Drake refused to leave her day or night, and then he decided that the safest place for her was in his bed!